PANIC AT EMU FLAT

Books by Robert Elmer

ADVENTURES DOWN UNDER

#1 / *Escape to Murray River*
#2 / *Captive at Kangaroo Springs*
#3 / *Rescue at Boomerang Bend*
#4 / *Dingo Creek Challenge*
#5 / *Race to Wallaby Bay*
#6 / *Firestorm at Kookaburra Station*
#7 / *Koala Beach Outbreak*
#8 / *Panic at Emu Flat*

THE YOUNG UNDERGROUND

#1 / *A Way Through the Sea*
#2 / *Beyond the River*
#3 / *Into the Flames*
#4 / *Far From the Storm*
#5 / *Chasing the Wind*
#6 / *A Light in the Castle*
#7 / *Follow the Star*
#8 / *Touch the Sky*

PROMISE OF ZION

#1 / *Promise Breaker*
#2 / *Peace Rebel*

Panic at Emu Flat

BETHANY HOUSE PUBLISHERS
MINNEAPOLIS, MINNESOTA 55438

Cover illustration by Chris Ellison
Cover design by Lookout Design Group, Inc.

Published by Bethany House Publishers
A Ministry of Bethany Fellowship International
11400 Hampshire Avenue South
Minneapolis, Minnesota 55438
www.bethanyhouse.com

Printed in the United States of America by
Bethany Press International, Minneapolis, Minnesota 55438

Library of Congress Cataloging-in-Publication Data

Elmer, Robert.
Panic at Emu Flat / by Robert Elmer.
p. cm. — (Adventures down under ; 8)
SUMMARY: While helping his family operate a paddle steamer along the Murray River in Australia during the 1860s, thirteen-year-old Patrick gets into serious trouble because of his friend.
ISBN 0–7642–2106–X
[1. Paddle steamers Fiction. 2. Friendship Fiction. 3. Australia Fiction.] I. Title. II. Series: Elmer, Robert. Adventures down under ; 8.
PZ7.E4794 Pan 1999
[Fic]—dc21 99–6560
CIP

To Brad, Brenda,

and their adventurous kids—

Megan, Jessie, and . . .

MEET ROBERT ELMER

ROBERT ELMER is the author of THE YOUNG UNDERGROUND series, as well as many magazine and newspaper articles. He lives with his wife, Ronda, and their three children, Kai, Danica, and Stefan (and their dog, Freckles), in a Washington State farming community just a bike ride away from the Canadian border.

CONTENTS

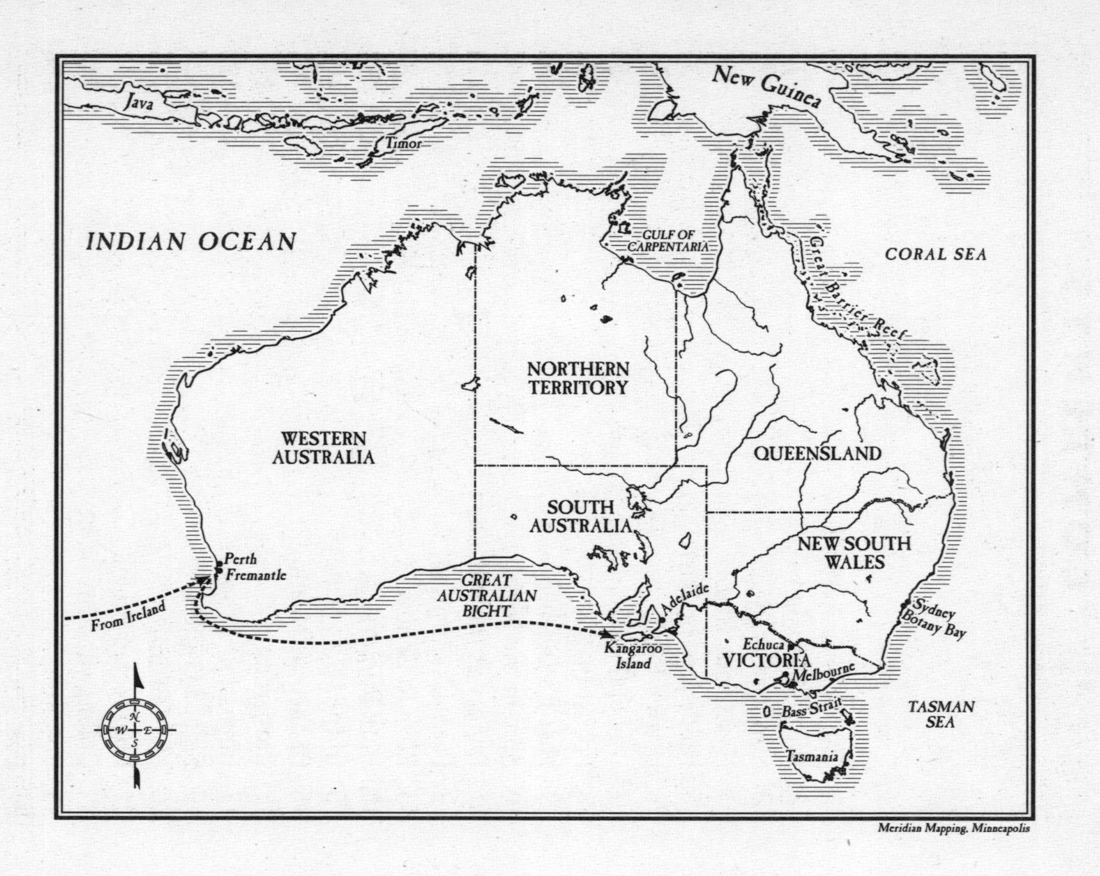

Meridian Mapping, Minneapolis

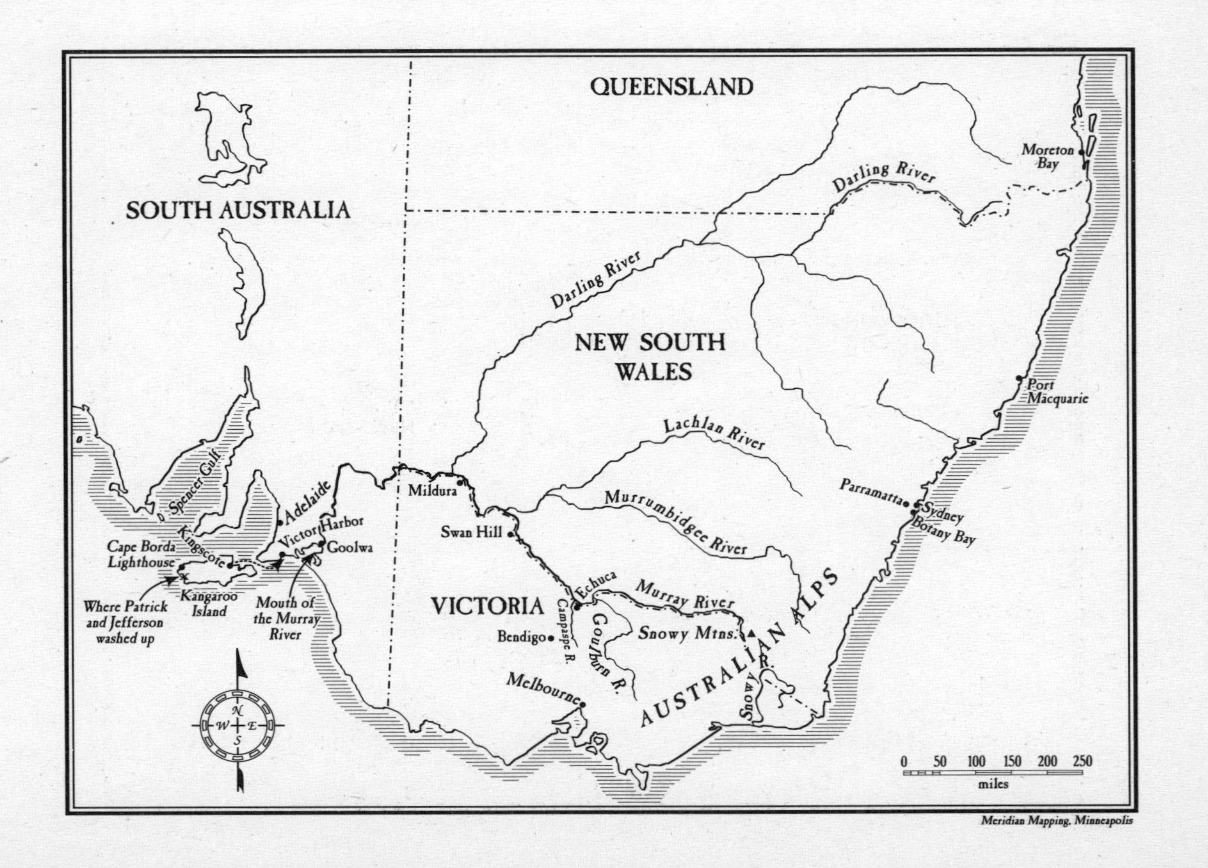

Meridian Mapping, Minneapolis

CHAPTER 1

THE *VICTORIA* RETURNS

"I don't care *what* you tell them, as long as you get these . . . these *things* off my boat!"

Thirteen-year-old Patrick McWaid stopped to listen to the man's complaints drifting down the wide, brown Murray river. He mopped the sweat from his brow and dropped one more wooden crate on the rear deck of his family's paddle steamer, the *Lady Elisabeth*. His sister, Becky, and their younger brother, Michael, also paused.

"And look at that *mess*!" screamed the man. He sounded a little clearer, a little closer. "You're going to clean up every last—"

"Taking a break this morning?" Patrick's father stepped up from behind them.

"No, sir." Patrick turned to see his red-bearded father, the captain of the *Lady Elisabeth* since Patrick's grandfather had died earlier that year. "We were just noticing the *Victoria* coming back to Goolwa already."

Patrick pointed at the grand, triple-decked paddle steamer bearing down on the Goolwa wharf with a full head of steam. The *Victoria*. All 120 feet of her. The finest appointments and fanciest passenger cabins on Australia's longest river. And so many shiny brass fittings that Patrick almost had to blink when the sun sparkled on the new ship. It was the same steamer the McWaids'

American friend Jefferson Pitney now served on as a crew member.

But Patrick didn't want to think about that just then. He knew he would only get mad again—mad at Jeff for deserting them and joining another crew. Never mind the better pay, or the chance to work on a "real" paddle steamer.

Traitor.

Instead, Patrick pressed his lips together and watched heavy black smoke billow out of the *Victoria*'s smokestacks. Then something on the foredeck caught his eye. It looked to Patrick like a fight.

"Hmm." Mr. McWaid crossed his arms across his lean, muscular frame and watched. "This ought to be interesting."

An officer on the approaching steamer sputtered and screamed a string of curses while another man scurried about trying to drape a canvas tarp over two huge crates on the forward deck. But the sailcloth kept billowing out and flapping in the breeze.

"I'm telling you, boy, I'm going to count to ten, and if those things aren't gone . . ."

Patrick couldn't hear what the poor sailor said in return. But there was no doubt who it was.

"Say, isn't that. . . ?" began Mr. McWaid. He, too, had noticed.

"That's Jeff, all right," answered Patrick. "I didn't recognize him at first, with that red- and white-striped shirt and that silly blue cap."

"I think he looks funny." Michael giggled. He was four years younger than Patrick and still giggled a lot.

"You hush," Becky scolded him and brushed her flowing red hair out of her eyes. "That's just the uniform he has to wear."

She frowned, as if thinking twice about what she had just said. "Although, if he had stayed with us here on the *Lady Elisabeth* where he belongs, he wouldn't have to wear such a thing."

"Well, uniform or no," said Patrick, stepping back a few feet, "Jefferson Pitney and the *Victoria* are going to crash into the wharf in a minute if they don't—"

"Whatever is wrong out there?" interrupted Patrick's mother. "It sounds as if there's a regular civil war going on."

Mrs. McWaid's mouth dropped open when she leaned out the door of the paddle steamer's salon. "Oh . . . my," she stammered, but there was nothing she could do to stop the disaster about to happen.

"Hello there! Hey!" Michael dropped the crates he was carrying and waved his arms over his head. "Slow down!"

"Michael!" Mrs. McWaid scolded her youngest son, dragging him back from the edge of the deck. "I'm sure they know what they're doing. Now, you just stay away from the edge of the boat."

"But, Ma!" protested Michael. "They're going to crash into the wharf, sure as day."

Patrick knew his brother was right. He turned his head away and wrinkled up his face, waiting.

It was almost as if the giant, triple-decked *Victoria* were intending to ram the poor old Goolwa wharf. And if it *were*, there was no doubt who would win the contest. The splintered old wharf was already sagging under the weight of too many heavy cargoes, and it usually shivered when Patrick bounced on the boards.

So it was no surprise when the *Victoria*'s front rail grated hard into a couple of rotted pilings at the edge of the wharf, which splintered and screeched in the late-morning air. The pilings bent to the point of breaking, then somehow managed to slowly push back.

"Hold her there!" cried the foulmouthed officer from the side deck. He couldn't have been older than twenty-five or thirty, but he looked as if he was in charge. He gripped the railing of his paddle steamer with one hand. With his blue, peaked officer's cap in the other, he gestured wildly for the steersman to keep the *Victoria* nudged nose-first into the wharf. And still the paddle wheels churned, sending up a fountain of cool river water.

"Nice landing, Jeff!" Michael waved at the *Victoria*, then grabbed the rope from the *Lady Elisabeth*'s loading crane. He swung across and landed with a tumble on the deck of the incoming paddle steamer.

"Michael, stay here!" Mr. McWaid was quick to grab for his son, but the noise from the paddle next to them and the shouting of the other captain drowned out nearly everything. He turned to Patrick.

"Patrick, go fetch your brother and make sure he doesn't get hurt."

"John." Mrs. McWaid's sunny expression clouded over. "We've told him dozens of times not to swing on that thing."

"I know, Sarah. Patrick?"

"I'm going." Patrick was tempted for just a moment to follow Michael on the crane swing, but he thought better of it. Instead, he hopped to the wharf and made his way through a maze of barrels over to the other boat. The long way around.

"Michael!" Patrick hollered in the direction his brother had taken. "You need to get back to the *Lady E.*"

But no one heard him, least of all Michael. He was in the middle of the action, helping the *Victoria*'s uniformed deckhands lift one of the enormous crates up to the wharf, just a bit higher than the main deck. Patrick figured the crate could have held two or three large pianos. And by the way the sailors were sweating and grunting, that's what very well could have been inside.

As the sailors worked, Patrick noticed fifteen or twenty passengers hurrying off the *Victoria*. Strange. He would have to ask Jefferson about that.

Jefferson wrestled with the crank of a deck crane, turning the handle as fast as he could. But still he seemed to be in trouble.

"HIGHER, I said!" The young officer mopped his forehead with a handkerchief, then folded it carefully and stuffed it back into the pocket of his thick, woolen navy blue jacket. He must not have been able to see Michael under the crate; Patrick was afraid of what he would say if he did.

"Michael." Patrick quietly tried to get his brother's attention—and not the officer's.

"Come on, Yank. It's just a few birds." The officer paced in a tight circle, pulled out his handkerchief once more, and glanced around nervously.

"I'm sorry, sir. M-maybe we'll need some help." Jefferson's arms bulged as he turned the crank, but it seemed to go slower and slower. "It's stuck, or . . . I don't know."

"Excuses!" A vein pumped on the side of the officer's forehead.

Patrick could see it clearly, even from where he stood on the edge of the wharf, at least ten feet away. He thought he heard the man's teeth grinding, too, but it must have been Jefferson's cranky crane.

"Patrick, come here!" From down on the deck, Michael lifted a canvas to one side and peeked into a second large crate through a row of grapefruit-sized holes in the side. "You have to see this."

"No, I don't," Patrick called back as softly as he could. "*You* have to get out of there. That other crate is going to fall on you, and—"

"What's that?" asked the officer. Jefferson had finally cranked his load high enough; it was time to swing it out closer to the wharf. "What's that urchin doing down there? Get him off my ship!"

Patrick jumped across to the deck of the other boat and scooped up Michael under his arm.

"Don't!" complained Michael. "I want to stay and help Jeff." He squirmed, but Patrick held fast. Fortunately, the officer had found someone else to yell at for the time being.

"Patrick," whispered Jefferson under his breath. "You'd best stay away."

The older boy looked as if he were concentrating on his crane. But when Jefferson glanced up at the officer for a moment, Patrick noticed a wide-eyed look of fear in his eyes—a look he'd never before seen on Jefferson.

"Jeff? Are you all right?"

"Never better," Jefferson told him as he tugged at his crane handle and shook the expression from his face. "Just don't let him see you talking to me."

"But he's so *mean*," piped up Michael.

Jefferson didn't answer. He looked like he was going to say something but changed his mind.

"Is he always yelling at you like that?" asked Patrick.

"You should get back to the *Lady Elisabeth*—now," Jefferson told him out of the corner of his mouth. "Don't worry about me."

"But you need help," insisted Michael.

"No, I don't. I'm fine. A man can handle this kind of thing."

"But what about *him*?" Patrick nodded up at the officer. The man looked like a thundercloud ready to burst.

"AREN'T YOU OFF MY SHIP YET?"

Patrick felt like telling the man to be quiet and have a little patience, but he thought better of it. He backed up slowly, his brother in tow.

"Go on." Jefferson motioned with his eyes for them to leave. "Maybe I'll see you up the river. I'll be all right."

Jefferson's expression told them just the opposite as Patrick dragged Michael back to the safety of the wharf. Their friend was definitely *not* all right.

"And STAY off!" screamed the officer. Patrick was sure he could see steam coming out of the man's ears. By that time Mr. McWaid had joined them on the wharf.

"See here, now, what's going on?" asked Mr. McWaid as Michael hid behind him. They had run into a few rough characters on the river before, but nothing quite like this.

"Nothing, Pa," whimpered Michael. "I was just looking at the ostriches in that crate."

"Pitney, if you see that little goblin again within ten feet of my vessel"—the officer pointed a long, bony finger at Michael and looked down a considerable nose—"I expect you to throw him into the river. Do you understand?"

"Yes, sir."

CHAPTER 2

NOT OLD ENOUGH

"Now, then," Mr. McWaid said sternly to the *Victoria*'s officer. He stood up straight but kept a firm hand on Michael behind his back. "I'll be sure to have my boys stay away from your cargo. But you needn't—"

"See that you do." The red-faced officer straightened the front bill of his cap and returned his glare to Jefferson. "And now you, Pitney, what are you staring at? I'm going to count to ten, and if these infernal beasts aren't off-loaded from my ship, I'll see a half month's pay from your pocket! We're going to depart this infernal place while it's still 1869, my friend."

He doesn't sound at all like a "friend," thought Patrick as he shivered at the steely tone of the officer's voice. Where had he come from? And the cargo—Patrick hadn't seen it go aboard when the *Victoria* left Goolwa just a day earlier.

"That Officer York is quite a character, isn't he?" came a soft voice from beside them. A man in the same striped uniform as Jefferson's grasped in his hands a thick rope, holding the paddle steamer in place. Patrick hadn't noticed him there on the wharf before.

"Is he always like that?" wondered Michael as the crate tipped their way.

"Only his first full day on the *Victoria*, but so far, yeh." The man's voice was barely above a whisper. "He's not shy, I'll say that for him."

As Officer York continued to holler, Patrick wished he could hide behind his father the way Michael did.

"That's right," the sailor continued. "They slipped him and the cargo in last night, real quiet, and then we left before first light."

"Is he the captain?" wondered Michael.

"First mate, but he's surely in command," answered the man. "That is, nobody ever sees our *real* captain, excepting when he comes out to complain about his ship being taken away from him. Captain Witherspoon was always a tough buzzard, but this Officer York is far worse."

"CAREFUL!" screamed Officer York. "You're going to break the crane, you clumsy . . ."

"Why does he shout so?" asked Patrick.

"Fresh off an oceangoing brigantine, they say." The sailor kept a careful eye out and his voice down. "Ex-navy, and acts the part. Maybe it's because his father is someone high up in the government, but I haven't heard the whole story as of yet. The Yank there, Pitney, is the only one who seems to know who he is."

"He does?" asked Patrick.

"That's what he said this morning. Turned white as a ghost when he first heard York's name mentioned. Of course, Officer York doesn't make a very good first impression on anybody."

"No," Patrick agreed. "He doesn't."

"Worst of it is he brought all these stinkin' uniforms with him so we could all look 'seagoing.' "

The man pulled and stretched the collar of his shirt; it looked far too small. Patrick had never seen anyone else on the river wearing anything like it. He felt itchy just looking at the man.

"But the ostriches," Michael wanted to know as they watched Jefferson lean into the crate. "What about the ostriches?"

"Michael, you must mean emus," Patrick corrected. "Remember we learned about emus in our school book? Emus are here in Australia. Ostriches are only in Africa."

"No, I think they're ostriches," answered Michael. "I know what emus look like. Ostriches are bigger, and they're a different color."

"The young lad's right," said the sailor, nodding at Michael. "Them's ostriches, all right. And big beasts, they are. Imported all the way from Capetown, South Africa. Bound for some kind of farm up the river, Echuca-way. Some fool's going to get rich selling feathers to fancy ladies."

"The second crate—NOW!" Officer York pulled out a stopwatch. "We've already lost a full day thanks to this."

"Ha," said the sailor under his breath. "You think the man's steamed now, you should have seen his face a few hours back. And they say he's even worse when he's found himself a bottle."

"Really?" Michael was following the man's story now, and the sailor nodded seriously.

"We'd better be going," said Mr. McWaid, taking his son's hand. Michael dug in his heels.

"Sailor," shouted Officer York. "We're off as soon as the Yank here unloads this second crate."

"Aye, sir." The sailor puffed up his chest and flexed his arms as if his rope-holding job were really important. Just as quickly he lowered his voice to continue his story.

"As I was saying, you should've seen him when one of those birds nearly swallowed his hand. Bit the captain, too, so it was the both of 'em. But York, he was just passing by the cage, and snap! He was mad as a March hare. His eyes bulged out like goose eggs, and he got all red in the face—even redder'n he is now."

"What then?" Michael was hooked. "Did he start yelling?"

"Yelling?" The man pointed at the officer with his chin. "You hear him now? He's just whispering, compared."

"Really?"

"I'm telling you the truth, lad. So that's when he orders the *Victoria* turned around on the spot. 'We are *not* ferrying these beasts all the way to Echuca,' he says. And I says, 'I don't care a hoot, as long as I collect my pay at the end of the month.' Lucky he knows how much money them birds cost, or he'd probably have strangled 'em and shoved 'em right off the deck."

"But what about your passengers?" wondered Michael. "Why did they leave?"

"Ha! Passengers!" The sailor chuckled. "Don't blame 'em for jumping ship. Officer York was hollering at 'em already before sunup. He most likely shooed them all off when he had us pile cargo in the hallways."

"In the hallways?" Patrick looked over his shoulder for the passengers who had escaped York's sharp tongue, but they were long gone.

"That's a fact." The sailor nodded. "Now, don't tell him I said so, but I don't think this Officer York cares for passengers, no more than he does for ostriches. Guess he'd rather just deal with bales of cotton and such, seeing as how they don't argue back."

"PUSH, would you!" Officer York clapped his hands together, as if that would have helped Jefferson secure the second crate of birds any faster. Now Patrick was starting to wonder what a real ostrich looked like up close.

"I'm trying, I'm trying," muttered Jefferson, leaning out from the deck of the *Victoria* as far as he could. The crane must have slipped a notch just then, or maybe the ostriches jumped. But the crate swayed and rocked, and Jefferson grabbed for the corner.

"Watch out, Jeff!" Patrick jumped to the edge of the wharf to give a hand.

"I've got it, thanks." Jefferson didn't even sound like Jefferson—none of the usual smiles or easy, soft way of talking.

Patrick looked around for help, but Michael and his father were now inspecting the first crate of ostriches a few yards away, up on the wharf. Becky was watching from the deck of the *Lady Elisabeth*, but the dark look on her face told him she wasn't coming any closer. Becky had always had a soft spot for Jefferson, and Patrick knew Jeff's leaving had hurt her more than any of them.

"Jeff?" Determined, Patrick tried to catch his friend's eye again. But Jefferson wouldn't look straight back at him. Officer York was too close. "We could still use you on the *Lady Elisabeth*, you know. Everybody wants you back."

Jefferson's muscles strained as he wrestled the corner of the second crate around to rest on the dock. He *did* notice Becky watching them, and he nodded up at her. She turned quickly away. But whatever he might have been thinking, he caught himself. “No. Too late for that,” Jefferson mumbled back. “I’m signed up for this crew now. And like I told you, a man like me can take a little hard work.”

“Pitney!” called the impatient officer. “You almost done?”

Jefferson squeezed his eyes shut for a moment, as if trying to decide something.

“Are you deaf, Pitney?” shouted Officer York, checking his pocket watch once more. “Now, get that boy out of the way, untie the rope, and let’s shove off.”

“Yes, sir.”

Patrick wanted to try one more time. He lowered his voice and rested his hand on Jefferson’s shoulder.

“I’m telling you, Jeff, it’s not too late. Something bad is bound to happen here.”

But the older boy froze under Officer York’s watchful eye. The other sailor—the one who had told them about Officer York—was standing nearby, too.

“PITNEY!” cried the officer.

“Yes, sir,” Jefferson quickly called back, shrugging off Patrick’s hand. “R-right away, sir.”

Fine. Patrick set his jaw. *If that’s the way he’s going to be . . .*

Ignoring the officer’s glare, Patrick attacked one of the knots in the thick rope that held the ostrich crate. He did his best to untie it the way he’d seen Jefferson do, but he only seemed to make the knot tighter and tighter. His fingers fumbled.

“You don’t know how to do sailor’s knots, Patrick.” Jefferson tried to reach in. “Let me handle it, will you?”

“No, let me try.” Patrick tried once more, but finally Jefferson pushed him aside.

“You know I don’t have time for this,” said the older boy, looking around nervously.

“I’m just trying to help, all right? Why don’t you let me help?”

“I don’t need your help, Patrick. You’re only making it worse.”

"Wait just a minute." Patrick's mouth was in motion before he knew what he was saying, and he grabbed at the knots again. "You needed my help when you fell overboard and I jumped into the ocean after you, remember? How about *that*?"

"That was a long time ago." Jefferson didn't look at Patrick and grabbed for the knot.

Patrick's face was hot. He grunted and slammed his fist as hard as he could at the jammed knot.

"You and that Irish temper of yours," Jeff declared. "When are you ever going to grow up?"

Patrick yanked fiercely at the tangled ropes. He hadn't meant to remind Jefferson about how they had nearly drowned on the long trip from Ireland to Australia. It wasn't something he liked to remember, either. Maybe it embarrassed Jeff to hear it again. But it had just slipped out of Patrick's mouth.

"I don't know why I'm even doing this," grumbled Patrick as he fussed with the rope. "I try to help and—"

"I'm telling you, Pitney, get rid of that kid." Officer York stared impatiently at them from above. "Or we're leaving you behind. Do I make myself clear?"

"You can't tell me you actually *like* working for that man," whispered Patrick. Jefferson ignored the comment.

"Coming, sir." Jefferson pulled a long sailor's knife out of his belt, scaled the side of the box like a monkey, and with one sawing motion sliced the rope free at the top. The large knot fell limply into Patrick's hands as he stood on the wharf. The other sailor, the storyteller, had already found his way back aboard the *Victoria*.

"Fine, then, don't tell me," fumed Patrick. He wound what was left of the rope around the knot until it looked like a giant ball of yarn. "You just do whatever . . . whatever you want. See what happens."

"You don't understand, Patrick." Jefferson hopped down to the *Victoria*'s deck and faced Patrick for a moment as he replaced the knife in his belt.

"Maybe I don't."

Already the boat's paddle wheels were churning backward, and the *Victoria* began inching away from the battered Goolwa wharf. Officer York pulled long and hard on the steam whistle as Jefferson turned and walked away.

"You forgot something!" yelled Patrick. He heaved the ball of rope as hard as he could straight at Jefferson. "Take your old rope with you!"

For one angry moment Patrick didn't care if it hit his friend or not. But it did. He gasped when Jefferson stumbled forward, caught himself, and gripped the back of his neck. It must have hurt.

The paddle wheels turned faster and faster. Jefferson didn't look back, just rubbed his neck and kicked the rope off the deck into the river. Without a word he disappeared through a door down into the paddle steamer.

Patrick stood there shaking, a part of him horrified at what he had done, another part still steaming like the *Victoria*'s whistle. He would have said, "I'm sorry," but of course it was far too late for that. And he wasn't even sure if he could have said it anyway.

Still, it would have been better if Jefferson had said something. Anything.

When am I going to grow up, he says? Patrick bit his lip to keep from crying. *I'll show* you, *Jefferson Pitney!*

"You there, boy." Officer York leaned back over the upper railing of his ship and pointed down at Patrick like a king pointing at a slave. "I saw that!"

CHAPTER 3

STRANGE CARGO

"Who, me?" Patrick wished he hadn't heard the man.

"Yeh, you," answered Officer York. He cupped his hands around his mouth to shout. "And if I ever catch you or your brother around my ship again, you'll be sorry you ever met me."

Too late for that, thought Patrick. He backed away from the edge of the wharf as if the man could reach a long arm across the water and grab him by the throat.

"And one other thing." Officer York wasn't going to let Patrick get away so easily. "Tell the shipping agent he can do whatever he likes with those infernal beasts. Just so long as they're not on my ship. Understand?"

Patrick felt himself nodding; he couldn't help it. Officer York didn't wait for an answer, just turned away to yell at another of his crew. At Jefferson, maybe. A thick cloud of wood smoke hit Patrick in the face, and he turned away, squeezing the tears from his eyes.

"Why did you talk like that to Jefferson?" Michael had finished inspecting the ostrich crates and looked up at Patrick as they stood on the edge of the wharf. Mr. McWaid was speaking to a couple of men on the wharf as the boys watched the *Victoria* disappear upriver. "I thought he was your friend."

"I thought so, too, Michael." Patrick watched where the piece of rope Jeff had cut sank into a wave. "I thought so, too."

"This is a disaster," fumed a man as he hurried to the edge of the wharf. He wiped his thick glasses on the sleeve of his starched white shirt, replaced them on his nose, and stared up the river. The glasses were too heavy for his nose, though, so they just kept slipping down.

Is he looking for something else? wondered Patrick. *Jefferson's boat is long gone.*

"I'm afraid there was nothing we could have done, Mr. Cribble," apologized Mr. McWaid, turning to the Goolwa shipping agent. "The *Victoria* just rushed in, unloaded the crates, and then they were off again. I thought about sending one of the children to fetch you, but it all happened so fast."

"I'm not blaming you," mumbled Mr. Cribble, but he looked as if he would cry. He rubbed his forehead over and over. "It's my job to see these kinds of things are sent on their way without any trouble. But I'll tell you, that York fella certainly didn't make a good impression on *me*."

"The sailor said we were lucky they didn't dump them in the river," said Michael, and Mr. McWaid signaled with his eyes for the boys to be quiet. Michael missed the signal and smiled back at him. "The ostriches, I mean. Pa, I *knew* it was ostriches the first time I saw them. Patrick said they had to be emus, but I knew better."

"Shh." Mr. McWaid held a finger to his lips. Becky finally joined them, coming over to see what they were talking about.

"I've been reading about them." Michael retreated to a spot on the wharf between the two ostrich crates. "Emus, you know."

Mr. McWaid smiled and nodded at his son.

"Oh, this is a fine mess." Mr. Cribble began to pace. His eyes looked odd—bulging, even—every time Patrick caught a glimpse of them. "I personally promised these expensive birds would be delivered on time. That was *days and days* ago, and now there's no other cargo boat available!"

"I'm sorry." Mr. McWaid shook his head.

"I'm not," whispered Michael.

"Michael, how can you say that?" Becky scolded. "This is serious."

"Maybe. But if the *Victoria* hadn't brought these ostriches back, we never would have seen them, right? Don't you think they're wonderful, Patrick?"

Patrick wasn't quite sure, but he didn't mind taking a look as the adults talked. One of the birds was close enough to the big row of breathing holes that they could see the magnificent black-and-white plumes sticking out. He could barely make out the funny long neck and the odd face with the wide beak and bulging eyeballs. Almost like Mr. Cribble's eyes!

"Patrick, we should stay away from them." Becky pointed at the row of breathing holes. "They look dangerous."

"I think they're just scared. I can hardly see them." Patrick could make out three ostriches in each of the crates. In one of the cages, two were huddled against each other while a third paced, its claws clicking on the wood floor. Black-and-white feathers pressed by the air holes, back and forth.

"That's what's so valuable about the birds, you know," said Michael, eager to tell them what he knew.

"Oh?" Patrick followed the movement of the pacing bird. The others were a bit smaller, probably younger.

"Sure. The feathers. For ladies' hats."

"I knew that."

"Well, I think they're pretty."

Patrick wasn't sure "pretty" was the best word for the ostriches. But they *were* unusual. And certainly big.

"I think the bird that's pacing is as worried as Mr. Cribble." Patrick perked up his courage and inched closer for a better look.

"I don't know what Mr. Cribble is so worried about." Michael had to stand on his tiptoes to reach the row of vents. "So the *Victoria* doesn't take the birds. Somebody else will."

"Hmm," said Patrick. "I think you just gave me an idea, Michael."

"Absolutely not," said Mr. McWaid less than an hour later. "For one thing, there's not room for them on deck. And for another, who would take care of them? We're already shorthanded as it is."

Patrick took a piece of string out of his pocket and gave one end to his brother. He pointed for Michael to stand on the foredeck, just in front of the main salon cabin.

"They fit. See, Pa?" Patrick took a couple of steps and pulled the string tight. "I measured the two crates. They look big, but they would fit right in here if we just moved a few things to the side."

Patrick's father frowned, while Mr. Cribble's face brightened for the first time all day.

"I believe he has a point, McWaid. I hadn't thought they would fit on your vessel here, but the boy is right."

"No, I don't think so, Mr. Cribble." Patrick's father held up his hands. "I'd like to help, but I'm afraid I know nothing of caring for exotic birds. I'd probably do more harm than good. And I'm sure there's a good reason the *Victoria* brought them back."

"But *I'd* care for them, Pa." Patrick hoped his father was softening. "There's only six of them. Three in each crate. I'd feed them every day until we got to Echuca. You won't have to worry about a thing. I promise."

Mr. McWaid gave his son a puzzled look. "What's got you so interested in six ostriches all of a sudden?"

"I just am, that's all," said Patrick. "I . . . I want to prove . . ."

His voice trailed away. He was going to say, "I want to prove I've grown up," but that would have sounded silly, or like a little boy. Or maybe like Jefferson Pitney. Instead, he just kept quiet.

Mr. McWaid stood on the deck with his hands on his hips, looking back and forth between the nervous shipping agent and Patrick.

"Please, Pa?" asked Michael.

"You'd be doing me a big service, McWaid." Mr. Cribble was doing everything but getting down on his knees. "At this point, anything is better than leaving them here on the wharf to die."

"I know I'm going to regret this," said Mr. McWaid with a big sigh. "Ah, what's there to do but take the birds?"

Mr. Cribble broke out in a smile and pumped Mr. McWaid's hand while Michael whooped.

"But *you*, young man." Mr. McWaid pointed seriously at Patrick, who wiped the grin off his face. "You'll have a big responsibility. For water, for food, and—" he paused—"for keeping these cages clean."

"Aye, aye, sir!" Patrick straightened his back and saluted his father. "The floors will be clean enough to eat on."

"Maybe for the birds," put in Mrs. McWaid, leaning out the window. "But certainly not for any of you."

"You can help, too." Mr. McWaid shifted his gaze to Michael. "Although, aren't you having a hard enough time lately with the koala? Where did he run off to now?"

"He's all right, Pa." Michael looked around for Christopher. Patrick couldn't remember the last time he had seen the little bundle of fur. Maybe he was off exploring the paddle steamer again.

"This is splendid." Mr. Cribble beamed. "Now, the only thing is, you must promise me you won't bring the birds back the way Officer York did. You'll only receive your pay for the shipment when the birds are delivered safely to Echuca."

"We'll take care of them fine, Mr. Cribble." Patrick patted the side of one of the crates. "We promise."

"You can depend on us," added Michael. Mr. McWaid nodded, too.

"I deeply appreciate it," answered the shipping agent. "But since the shipment is already late, I would also appreciate if you could proceed with all haste to Echuca."

"We'll be doing the best we can, sir," replied Mr. McWaid. "Come on, boys, let's clear a space for these birds."

But they were stopped in their tracks at the sound of a heavily accented woman's voice.

"Set it down on the deck, young man!" Patrick looked up to see a tall, prim woman in a serious black dress directing the operator of a wharf crane as he swung a large barrel over the bow of the *Lady E*. "Down right there, see?"

"Wait a minute!" protested Mr. McWaid. "We've barely enough deck space for the confounded ostriches. Is this their food, I assume?"

"Uh . . . not exactly." Mr. Cribble's smile had now vanished. "I hesitate to say . . . but truth be told . . . I've had a bit of trouble finding a place for this cargo, as well. I was hoping that since you were kind enough to help me with the live cargo, you wouldn't mind a few extra small barrels. And well, perhaps I've presumed upon you . . ."

"It's feast or famine." Mr. McWaid closed his eyes and shook his head. "Aye, the McWaids take anything, is that it? Put it anywhere. On my bunk, perhaps? There'll be no need of sleeping, what with these feathered passengers."

Mr. Cribble laughed at the joke as workers lowered the new cargo onto the forward deck of the *Lady Elisabeth*, just below the wheelhouse, on the left side. And after the three crates of birds, the barrels kept coming. Four, five, a half dozen . . .

"Vatch your head, young man!" The woman pointed down at Mr. McWaid, who stepped aside to let a barrel settle to the deck. "There's more vhere that comes from!"

"Of course." Patrick's father had given up the fight. He looked at the shipping agent. "And who might this be, Mr. Cribble?"

"Captain McWaid, meet Miss Perlmutter."

MYSTERIOUS GUEST

"*Pear*lmutter, young man." The woman in the black dress came down the ladder to the deck much more quickly than Patrick would have imagined. But she put out her hand for Mr. Cribble to help her down the last step, as if for show. "*Pear*, as in the fruit, you know?"

Patrick had to listen carefully to understand the woman's strong German accent.

"Yes, of course." Mr. Cribble bowed slightly, as he might have for royalty. "Miss Perlmutter, I'd like you to meet the captain of the *Lady Elisabeth*, John McWaid, and his family. John, this is Miss Perlmutter. She . . . uh . . . comes with the cargo."

Miss Perlmutter shook hands as if she were milking a cow back in Bavaria, with a little bow and a hard squeeze. Her clear, blue-eyed stare drilled into Patrick so hard that he had to look away. When he did, though, Miss Perlmutter wouldn't let go of his hand.

"You look like an intelligent young lad," she told him, still holding on. "You've read Goethe, I presume?"

Goethe? Patrick couldn't pronounce it if he tried, but it sounded something like *Grr-tuh*. He looked over at his sister for a clue. She had come down from the wheelhouse to meet the new passenger.

"I don't think so, ma'am." Patrick finally managed to slip his hand away from her lock grip. "I don't read German very well."

"Or not at all, I imagine." Miss Perlmutter squinted and pressed her lips together. "Ve shall have to change that. But vhat of the other classics? Plato, perhaps, or Aristotle. Surely them? In English?"

"Well . . ."

Miss Perlmutter leaned closer, and Patrick swallowed.

"I've been reading *Robinson Crusoe,*" he admitted quietly.

"Robinson Crusoe!" The woman gasped as if he had just splashed cold water on her face. "Ve shall have to do something about that. I have books vith me. Good books. You vill learn proper literature."

I will? wondered Patrick. No one had said anything about an on-board tutor. But she was kind of fun to listen to. Miss Perlmutter pronounced each word carefully, as if reading them slowly from the dictionary. *Literature* was "LEET-ehr-ah-toor," and when she said *proper*, she gargled the *r* way back in her throat, like "prrrr-oppah."

"Oh, you have books?" Becky sounded interested. "I love to read."

"I'm delighted to hear that." The woman smiled at Becky. "In Bavaria, vhen I vas a little girl, I read many good books. German books, English books, even Latin. Come see. In my baggage."

Becky and Miss Perlmutter would be getting along just fine, Patrick could tell. But he still wasn't quite sure what to think of her. The German woman looked back up to the wharf and signaled to the crane operator still waiting among her many wooden barrels.

"You may lower the rest of my things now, young man."

So it was official. Miss Perlmutter would be traveling with them. It didn't look as if Mr. McWaid had a choice.

"I'll show her inside, Pa," volunteered Becky. Miss Perlmutter put her hand up.

"*Nein*. No. Captain, I von't be requiring a room. I prefer sleeping out vhere I can get plenty of fresh air."

"You're certain?" Mr. McWaid looked puzzled, and Patrick knew why. They could hardly see the deck between the barrels and the ostriches and everything else.

"Absolutely, *Herr* Captain. Vas I not clear? I am accustomed to much vorse. Vhy, up in Neuperlmutterberg, many of the young people and I, ve still sleep under *Gottes Himmel*. Ve vatch shooting stars. It is *glorious*."

"What's a 'himmel'?" wondered Michael. "And where's *Noy* . . . whatever it was?"

"*Him*mull," pronounced Miss Perlmutter. When she crouched down to look Michael in the eye, Patrick realized for the first time that she was nearly as tall as his father. "Heaven. You believe in heaven, don't you? And that Jesus is vaiting for you there?"

Michael nodded quietly, his eyes wide.

"Good." She seemed satisfied with his answer. "Good boy. And vhat about your older brother?"

"Oh, he reads his Bible," explained Michael. "But I think he gets mad at God a lot."

"Michael!" Patrick grabbed his brother's arm to keep him quiet. Just then the men lowered Miss Perlmutter's trunk to the deck with a *thud*.

"Be careful of that luggage, young man!" she raised her voice, turned, and pointed at the dock worker. Patrick silently thanked the man for taking the attention away from what Michael had been saying about him.

"Are you coming with us, Miss Murlputter?" whispered Michael. Somehow she had charmed him, and he was hanging on every word she said. Even so, he looked afraid to get too close—as if she would bite.

"*Ja*, I vill. But first you are going to learn how to say my name correctly. Now—"

"Miss Perlmutter is coming along with this shipment of grain," interrupted the shipping agent. "It's for the German colony where she lives, upriver at Emu Flat. Isn't that right, Miss Perlmutter?"

"Emu Flat, Emu Flat!" complained the woman, straightening up. "Vhat is it vith you English? Always Emu Flat! Ve are a day upstream from Emu Flat, I vant you to know. And my father's last vish before he died vas that the German settlement be called Neuperlmutterberg. Could you not honor his memory by using the correct name?"

Now she was a tutor once more.

"Of course, ma'am," gulped Mr. Cribble. "If only I could pronounce it. Until then . . ."

"And you vill explain to them that this is not just any shipment of grain. Vhile ve stand here chatting, my people are fighting a plague of locusts and running out of food to eat. There are children up there in Neuperlmutterberg, you know."

"I heard about the locusts," put in Patrick. "One of the dock workers who was talking about it said you could cross the river on 'em and not get your feet wet."

Miss Perlmutter shook her head. "Those are just river stories. But still, it is awful, and the people are vaiting for the grain. These barrels must be delivered, and very soon. They go hungry."

"Well, then, if all the birds are loaded," said Mr. McWaid, "let's go!"

Mr. Cribble turned to leave as their new passenger found her place on deck. But the shipping agent felt his vest pocket and stopped.

"Oh, I almost forgot, Mr. McWaid." He pulled out a wrinkled envelope and held it out to Patrick's father. "Letter arrived for you the other day. I said I'd deliver it. And look here . . ." The man pointed to several handwritten notes on the face of the envelope. "Looks as if it's been from Melbourne to Echuca and now down here. It's been following you, it has."

Patrick studied the letter as he ferried it from Mr. Cribble over to his father. Perhaps it *was* odd that the Echuca postmistress hadn't held on to the letter, although she *did* know where they were. His eyes grew wide when he turned over the envelope and noticed the return address in neat block letters on the back.

"It's from Dublin, Pa!"

"Must be important, then?" wondered the shipping agent, rocking on his heels, looking over Patrick's shoulder. He bent to tie his shoelace, which wasn't untied. They all waited silently for Mr. McWaid to carefully slit the letter open with his pocketknife, unfold the two sheets of onionskin paper, and read the message.

Dublin! thought Patrick, and for a moment he let his mind wander back to the streets he had once known so well. He thought of the fruit sellers at the Bull Alley Market, the fishmongers, and the organ-grinder with his monkey. The taste of ripe plums he bought with the extra penny his father sometimes gave them. And he remembered the grand old buildings on Middle Abbey Street, near his father's office at the *Evening Telegraph*.

He smiled at the memories, but it seemed so far away and so long ago. Had it really been only two years?

"Well?" asked Mr. Cribble, dusting his trousers. "Good news?"

Mr. McWaid wiped the grin off his face, but Patrick could tell it was. His father looked over at Mrs. McWaid.

"It's from the owner of the *Evening Telegraph* himself, dear," he told her.

Mrs. McWaid looked confused. "Why would someone that important be writing to *us*?"

"He's finally apologizing for the entire horrible affair with Burke," continued Patrick's father, re-reading the lines.

"Well, it's about time, I say." Mrs. McWaid crossed her arms, but her husband held up his hand and moved the letter closer.

"Says, 'I deeply regret the way you were falsely accused and the pain your imprisonment must have caused.' "

"Oh." Mrs. McWaid put a hand to her lips. Not so long ago the memory would have brought tears to her eyes. "I didn't think the owner even knew what had happened."

Mr. McWaid focused on the letter and continued reading. "And then he says, 'It's my sincere hope that you will be able to return immediately to Dublin with your family and resume your career here at the *Evening Telegraph*. I would be happy to arrange for your passage and cover all expenses, and . . .' "

The news hit like a bomb out of the blue sky. Patrick could almost hear everyone's jaws dropping.

"We're not going to do it, are we?" Michael finally asked, as if they were talking about moving to the moon. "You're going to tell them no, aren't you?"

"*This* is our home," added Becky, looking out at the river.

But Mr. McWaid was far away, as far away as Patrick had been just a minute before, daydreaming about Dublin. He didn't answer Michael's question.

"Aren't you, Pa?" repeated Michael.

"What?" Mr. McWaid shook his head and looked down at them. He was still grinning.

"He said you're going to tell them no," said Becky. "Aren't you?"

"Well . . ." Mr. McWaid carefully folded the letter and replaced it in the envelope. "We don't have to answer for a few weeks. I can post a letter from Echuca. Don't you worry about a thing."

Patrick noticed his father hadn't exactly answered the question.

"Imagine that, Sarah," Mr. McWaid said to his wife as the two of them disappeared into the *Lady Elisabeth*'s salon. "It says here that O'Rourke is finally retiring after all these years, and now they want *me* to be the managing editor! *Managing editor!* Bring me back from halfway across the world, all expenses paid! And do you have any idea what they pay such a position?"

"Of *course* I'm not scared of her," Patrick whispered to his brother the next morning. He peeked over Michael's shoulder. "She's just so *odd*, don't you think?"

Becky looked back over her shoulder at them with a finger to her lips. "Shh!" Like a gatekeeper she stood quietly in front of the small space between two ostrich crates and all the grain barrels. Barrels were piled two and three high in a little ring on the forward deck of the *Lady E*. If Miss Perlmutter hadn't taken the space, it would have been the perfect spot for a hideout. But of course Patrick was too old for that, he reminded himself.

Now Michael hid behind his sister, and Patrick behind him. Their father was guiding the *Lady Elisabeth* along a straight, deeper portion of the river. Soon enough it would narrow down and start winding like a snake. But not yet.

Their dog, Firestorm, showed up just then, pausing at Patrick's ankles. The brown and gray fur on the back of his neck stood up, and Patrick heard a low growl.

"You feel the same way I do, boy," whispered Patrick.

"Shh!" Becky made a point of turning around and glaring at Patrick. "She'll hear you say that."

Sure enough, she did.

"Who is vhispering out on the deck?" asked Miss Perlmutter. Her voice boomed over the constant *swish, swish* of the paddle wheels. Patrick wasn't sure how she had heard them. "Come in here at once."

"Now we're in real trouble," whispered Patrick. He started to tiptoe in after the other two but changed his mind. No, he would stay at the opening—just in case.

Hidden in the Barrel

“Oh, this is a nice room,” said Becky, looking around the circle of barrels and crates and smiling at their new passenger. “And open to the fresh air, too. We were just curious—”

“We wanted to see what your hideout looked like!” blurted Michael.

“My hideout, ja.” Miss Perlmutter looked just a little amused as she sat on one end of the brown canvas cot she had been given to sleep on. A blanket was neatly folded and bundled at the other end, and her considerable trunk was opened to show more neatly bundled packages, many wrapped in brown paper and tied carefully with string. They reminded Patrick of the woman herself: plain, neatly bundled, tied back. But what was inside?

“For the people at the colony,” she said, motioning toward the trunk with a nod. “You didn’t really think a little old lady like myself vould need to carry so many things just for a trip to Goolva, did you?”

Old, maybe, thought Patrick. *But not little.*

“I . . . uh . . .” began Becky. “That is to say, we didn’t know what they were.”

“Of course not.” Miss Perlmutter was warming up again. “And that is exactly my point. You do not know many things. So I teach you.”

She patted the cot next to her. "Sit, young people. First I vill show you some of my books."

Patrick wasn't so sure, and he held back with Firestorm. It was the first time Patrick could remember the dog not running up to greet a new person with a friendly lick and a wag of his tail.

But Becky sat down next to Miss Perlmutter right away, ready for a lesson. Michael, meanwhile, had already found something else interesting.

"I wonder what this is for?" Michael slowly opened one of the small doors in the side of the ostrich crate. Patrick hadn't seen it before, but he guessed it looked like a floor-level feeding door. He made a mental note of it, since he would have to give the birds their first feeding today.

"Michael, don't!" warned Becky. "I think that's how Officer York was bit—"

"Yow!" Michael slammed the door and popped the finger into his mouth as he stumbled backward and into his sister's lap. Firestorm yapped and growled.

"Your first lesson, young man." Miss Perlmutter pulled out a book. "Never reach into dark places vhere you cannot see. Not if you value your fingers."

"I didn't know the birds would see me." Michael slid off to his own spot on the cot, and he still rubbed his hand. "That hurt."

"Of course it did." Miss Perlmutter stared down the mixed-breed shepherd dog until it whimpered back between Patrick's ankles.

Firestorm quietly growled, and she pointed at him.

" 'Am I vith thee my room to share,' " she recited, " 'poodle, thy barking now forbear, forbear thy howling!' "

"But that's not a poo—" began Michael, but Becky elbowed him in the ribs as Miss Perlmutter went on.

" 'Comrade so noisy, ever growling, I cannot suffer here to dvell, one or the other, mark me vell, forthvith must leave the cell.' "

Arf! replied Firestorm. But he seemed to understand her odd words and left the "room," snuffling and complaining.

"How did you do that?" wondered Michael.

"Goethe," she replied, pulling out a book and leafing through the pages. There was that German name again. "I just recited a few lines from Goethe. The mongrel understands fine literature."

Patrick wasn't sure about the "mongrel" understanding Goethe. *But if Firestorm is anything like me,* he thought, *that look of hers gives him chills.*

So Patrick continued to hold back, not saying anything, not sitting on the cot. Miss Perlmutter told them about Goethe and Aristotle. About ancient Greeks and famous people of history.

When it was her turn, Becky shared how since it was June 3, their friend Jefferson Pitney was probably celebrating Jefferson Davis's birthday.

"Jefferson Davis." Miss Perlmutter nodded. "The famous American general."

"He was president of the Confederacy during the American Civil War," answered Becky. "Our friend Jeff, well, he wasn't exactly named after Jefferson Davis, but I think he likes to say that he was."

"Except that he and Patrick had a fight over the ostriches," put in Michael. "That was just before you came."

"We did not, Michael." Patrick finally found his voice. "It wasn't about ostriches."

"Then why did you get so mad at him?" Michael wanted to know. "Your ears were steaming."

"It was just because he . . ." Patrick had tried to explain it to himself, but now he wasn't quite sure. "It was just that . . . he always thinks he's so old and wise."

"He *is* three years older than you." Becky sounded logical. Becky always did.

"Only two years and ten months," Patrick snapped back. "I'm going to be fourteen pretty soon, remember?"

"Ah, so I take it that you are grown-up and mature?" Miss Perlmutter looked impressed. Patrick wasn't sure how to answer. It was probably a trick.

"Well . . ."

"Of course you are. 'Vhen I vas a child, I spoke as a child, I understood as a child, I thought as a child. But vhen I became a man, I put avay childish things.' "

She stared at him with a gentle hint of a smile, as if daring him to argue. Patrick swallowed. He recognized the Bible verse but couldn't remember exactly where it was from. He made a silent note to himself to look it up later.

"Perhaps, then, this argument you had vith your friend . . . ist a little childish?" This time Miss Perlmutter raised her eyebrows as if she expected an answer. "Something to put avay?"

A little childish? fumed Patrick, but still he kept silent. *What does she know? And besides, I didn't come here to talk about Jefferson.*

He backed up a couple of steps and bumped into one of the barrels. The top must have been loose, though, and as he leaned back, he knocked the round wooden end to the deck.

"Don't vorry about that," began Miss Perlmutter.

But Patrick froze when he glanced down. A thick, polished wood handle barely poked up through the yellow-white grain. He wanted to pull it out to make sure, but there was really no doubt. It was a rifle, the end that would rest against a shooter's shoulder.

For a moment he didn't know what to say. He could pick up the wooden top, replace it, and pretend he hadn't seen anything. Or he could turn back to the steely-eyed Miss Perlmutter to demand the truth. Instead, he backed out of her room, tripping over the dog.

"I have to go," he mumbled. "I think it might be my turn to steer."

"Perhaps it was part of the barrel you saw," guessed Mr. McWaid later on. "I mean, the grain barrel, not the gun barrel."

He poked his head out the side of the wheelhouse to get a better view around the next bend in the river. "I simply can't imagine anything so sinister about Miss Perlmutter. She seems like such a fine, upstanding Christian woman."

"That's just it, Pa. Becky and Michael think she's wonderful. But . . ."

"But you're not so sure?"

"Maybe she's a spy for the kaiser."

"The kaiser!" Mr. McWaid laughed. "That sounds like something Michael might say when he's making up a story. Why would the German ruler need a spy in Australia, of all places?"

Patrick twirled his finger through his red hair. Of course it was silly. But he knew what he had seen, even if the rest of his family didn't believe him. It was definitely a rifle.

"Can't we at least ask her?" he tried once more.

Mr. McWaid looked over at his son with a little smile. "You know yourself how odd it sounds. But if you're that concerned about it, you're perfectly free to ask Miss Perlmutter about the gun you think you saw in the barrels."

Patrick sighed and turned to go.

"Actually, son, it's probably going to have to wait until after supper tonight. We should be close to Mannum fairly soon. I'm hoping they have a part there that I need for the steam engine. Becky and Miss Perlmutter are coming with me into town, as well."

"Miss Perlmutter, too?" echoed Patrick, but his father didn't look as if he was going to explain very much.

"That's right. But I'd like you and Michael to stay aboard."

"I know." Patrick could finish his father's sentence. "And stay out of trouble."

"Exactly." Mr. McWaid gave Patrick's shoulder a friendly squeeze as the town of Mannum finally came into view—the first town upriver from Goolwa.

It was busier here than Patrick had remembered. Maybe the train had just arrived from Adelaide, since people with boxes and wheelbarrows had crowded the small wharf. Becky had climbed to the side of the wheelhouse for a better look.

"I don't see it," she announced, shading the late afternoon sun with her hand.

Patrick knew she meant the *Victoria*. He sighed and wondered when they would see Jefferson again—or if he even wanted to.

"Don't worry. We know how to boil potatoes," Patrick assured the others as they stepped across to the wharf. Mr. McWaid gave his wife, daughter, and Miss Perlmutter a hand.

"Make sure Michael helps you." Mrs. McWaid checked to see that Patrick understood her. "We'll be right back."

"Yes, ma'am." Patrick looked over his shoulder at the small pile of potatoes he was supposed to peel and wash before supper. "Come on, Michael."

On potato number seven, though, Patrick dropped his knife.

"How could I forget?" he told his brother. Michael was putting plates on the table in the middle of the salon. Six plates, six knives, six forks. He looked up at Patrick.

"They're gone." Patrick pointed his knife at Michael. "Miss Perlmutter's gone. Now's my chance to see what's really in those barrels."

Michael studied his older brother for a moment, set down his plate, and shook his head slowly.

"I don't know, Patrick. I don't think there's anything wrong with Miss Perlmutter. She's been teaching us German words. Look. This is a *Kartoffel*. That's the word for *potato*, and—"

"All right, fine, Michael. I didn't say there was anything *wrong* with her. But look, we'd better hurry, before anyone gets back. I just want to make sure I really saw what I think I saw."

Michael followed Patrick's lead but stayed behind when they got to the ostrich cages.

"I'll keep watch out here," Michael said.

"Fine." Patrick nodded and slipped in to look at the barrels. His heart pounded in his ears.

"They're awfully quiet, don't you think, Patrick? I hope they're all right."

Patrick paused. What was Michael talking about now?

"You mean the ostriches?" he answered. "They're all right. I just fed them after lunch."

"I'm not so sure. I'm going to check on them."

Patrick glanced back to see Michael balancing on a piece of firewood, pressing his face to see through the holes in one of the crates.

"Fine," he told Michael. "Just don't let one of them bite you on the nose."

When Patrick turned back to the barrels, he felt a little guilty, as if he shouldn't be there. But he was, and he knew he didn't have much time. So he scrambled around inside Miss Perlmutter's makeshift room and tried the tops of a couple of barrels.

He knew the German woman would soon return to the paddle steamer. She wasn't one to waste time. He would have only a few minutes to find out about the guns she was smuggling in the grain barrels.

"Which one was it?" he asked himself aloud. It shouldn't have been so hard to find.

"Paa-trick!"

"What?" Patrick sighed and rolled his eyes. "Can you wait just a minute?"

"I don't think so. This latch is stuck."

"Latch?" Patrick caught his breath. "I hope you're not playing with the doors on those cages."

"I wasn't playing." Michael's voice sounded very soft and slightly guilty, as if he were confessing a crime. "I was just checking to see if they have enough food. You need to help me close this thing. It won't close."

"Listen . . ." Patrick worked at one of the barrel lids to get it open, but it wasn't cooperating. "Just keep watch, and I'll be right there."

A moment later Michael's voice sounded smaller still. It didn't sound good. Maybe it was the way he said "uh-oh."

"What now?" asked Patrick.

"She's coming back down the street!"

Patrick knew exactly whom his brother meant.

CHAPTER 6

OSTRICH PANIC

"Already?" Patrick almost broke a fingernail trying to get the top of a barrel loose.

"Patrick!" reported Michael. "She's almost to the wharf."

Patrick bit his lip. *One more*. And then the top of the next barrel popped free, but so did a cloud of flour.

"Oh no!" he whispered. "I thought these were all just grain. What a mess!"

But he had already come this far. He looked back over his shoulder, expecting to see the black-stockinged foot of Miss Perlmutter come over the edge of the wharf at any moment. He replaced the top of the flour barrel as best he could and tried one more.

"This is the one," he cried, and he plunged his arm into the grain.

"Where is it?" he wondered, fishing around. Nothing.

"Patrick!" hissed Michael.

"Right." Patrick slammed the top back on the barrel and did his best to kick the spilled grain to the side. It was all he could do.

He clapped his hands together, hoping the flour from the other barrel wouldn't show on his pants and shirt. But Patrick wasn't prepared for what happened next.

"No, wait!" cried Michael.

Patrick flew back out to the deck just in time to see the side door of the ostrich crate swing open and Michael tumbling backward.

"What are you doing?" demanded Patrick. "Close it!"

Michael did try, but he was too late. The bird must have seen its chance. In a flash of black-and-white feathers, the largest of the ostriches came charging out of its prison like a racehorse out of the gate, sending Michael crashing into a stack of firewood.

"I was just trying to help," croaked Michael. Patrick made a desperate grab at the ostrich, but it was quicker than he. Taller, too, and much larger-looking outside the cage.

"Himmel!" cried Miss Perlmutter from where she stood at the edge of the wharf. "*Vas ist das?*"

In the panic of the moment, she had switched back to speaking German, but the ostrich wasn't listening to any language. Patrick could see *freedom* written all over the big bird's bulging eyes. The ostrich was not going to waste its chance.

"Don't let it get away!" yelled Patrick, but what good would it do? The bird chose that moment to spring away from the cage and straight at Miss Perlmutter on the wharf. Maybe it was her black dress and her squawk that fooled the bird into thinking she was another ostrich.

"Ach, du Lieber!" cried Miss Perlmutter. As the bird launched out at her, she did the only thing she could do: cover her face and scream. The open crate in her arms went flying, sending cabbages and a plucked chicken spinning into the air.

The ostrich paused for just a moment—just long enough for Patrick to take a flying leap at its back. He came up with feathers and part of a wing, but it was just enough to hold on to as the terrified bird bolted across the Mannum wharf and into the dirt street.

"Stop, you!" Patrick pleaded with the big bird.

But the ostrich raced on, more than strong enough to drag Patrick through the street at a respectable trot. Patrick half ran, half dragged his heels, trying to slow the terrified animal. He was sure everyone in town was staring at them, but it was all he could do just to hang on.

"Please, bird," Patrick pleaded, and with one hand he grabbed the big cream-colored neck. "I'll give you extra supper. Just stop!"

The ostrich flapped its awkward wings and protested as if its life depended on escaping Patrick's grip. But Patrick wasn't giving up. With a mighty heave and a bounce, he flopped up on the bird's wide back and hugged the ostrich neck with both arms. Now he was able to balance a leg on either side to hold his position. Not very comfortable, but at least Patrick was on top now.

The ostrich must have taken this as a signal to *go!* and they raced down Mannum's narrow streets, dodging horses and well-meaning men who held up their hands to stop them. But the men would have had better luck flagging down the express train from Adelaide. Patrick, on his out-of-control ostrich, ran circles around a wagon, upsetting the horses and throwing a man through the air and into a cart of eggs, which promptly tipped over. As villagers slipped and slid on the smashed eggs and the ostrich charged on, Patrick heard his father's voice.

"Patrick! Stop that bird!"

Patrick wished he could. "I . . . I'm t-trying." He would just have to hold on until the ostrich ran out of steam. . . .

Patrick was afraid to hang on, but still more afraid to let go. Four men approached and hemmed them in—two standing in front with their arms held out, and two in back. They held the ostrich in position long enough for Mr. McWaid to slip a noose around its long neck and hold it still.

"It's all right, Patrick," reported Mr. McWaid. "We've got the big fella now."

"Are you sure?" Patrick eased off his feathered saddle, and his father helped him slide to the ground. The ostrich gave him a look, as if it had been wondering about the weight on its back, and Patrick patted the animal gently.

"There you go, boy," he cooed.

"You'd better explain exactly what is going on here, young man." Mr. McWaid did not sound at all pleased. The ostrich yanked at its noose.

"Oh, did you think. . . ?" Patrick began to explain, looking for the right words to say. It certainly looked bad, now that he had a chance to think about it. "I didn't . . . I mean, I really didn't want to do this, and it's not what it seems, Pa."

"Then you'd better make it clear for me." Mr. McWaid crossed his arms.

"Michael and I were making supper, like Ma asked us to," Patrick began. "Well, actually, we were out on deck and—"

"Stop right there. First you can explain what you were doing out on deck when you were supposed to be fixing the evening meal."

"Of course, Pa, but Michael thought the bird needed some more food. . . ."

"I thought that was your job."

"Well . . . it is." Patrick held up his hands. It was sounding worse all the time. "He wasn't trying to cause trouble. He just . . ."

Now Michael came running up the street.

"Patrick! There you are!" He squirmed his way through the knot of people who had gathered around to watch the ostrich. "Sorry I didn't come right away. I was helping Miss Perlmutter."

"She's all right?" Mr. McWaid wanted to know.

"Her groceries spilled all over the wharf. But, Patrick, that was great, the way you rode that thing. Like a racehorse. Can I try?"

"We are *not* going to be doing any more riding today," declared Mr. McWaid. He thanked the men for their help and pulled the ostrich back to the *Lady E*. "You boys have to be more careful. You simply don't seem to understand how valuable this bird is."

"We understand, Pa." Patrick hoped *something* he said would keep them out of trouble. "That's why I grabbed it."

"I thought he was going to drag you all the way to Sydney!" exclaimed Michael.

"Well, this might not have happened," scolded their father, "if you boys had been doing your chores the way you'd been told."

Miss Perlmutter was waiting for them back at the *Lady Elisabeth*.

"Mr. McVaid!" She frowned but kept a respectable distance. "Ve have a serious problem here."

"If you mean your spilled groceries," said Mr. McWaid as he led the ostrich back onto the deck of the paddle steamer, "I'm very sorry about that. Perhaps I'll have to put a lock on the cages from now on."

"That's not vhat I meant. Something—or someone—has been into my cargo."

"Oh?" replied Mr. McWaid. "You'll have to show me, then."

The barrels! Patrick dusted off his pants one more time, just to make sure all the flour was gone, then quietly followed his father and the ostrich to the afterdeck.

"I need to find Christopher," Michael told them and skipped away.

"Pa." Patrick tugged on his father's sleeve.

"Later, Patrick."

"But, Pa." Patrick didn't give up. He whispered into his father's ear. "*I* was the one in the barrel. I was looking for the gun. Remember I told you about it?"

Mr. McWaid slammed the door to the ostrich cage and looked from his son to Miss Perlmutter. With the ostrich safely back where it belonged, she finally stepped closer.

"Let me show you," she insisted. "Perhaps it's rats, though I don't see—"

"No, Miss Perlmutter, it wasn't rats." Mr. McWaid nodded his head slowly, as if waking up from a bad dream. "Apparently it was my son. Is that what you were trying to tell me, Patrick?"

Patrick nodded seriously.

"You?" Miss Perlmutter turned her attention to Patrick, as if she couldn't believe it. "Vhat vere you doing. . . ?"

"I'm very sorry, Miss Perlmutter." Patrick wiped his sweaty palms on the side of his pants, trying to think of the right thing to say. "But I saw something in your barrels this morning when the top came off, and—"

"Oh, is *that* vhat happened?" she interrupted. Her eyes narrowed, and she stepped up to face Patrick. Then she looked around the deck, making sure no one else could hear. "Vhat did you think you saw? A rifle, perhaps?"

"I . . . uh . . ." Patrick gave up trying to explain and nodded silently, not sure what to think. The strange old woman pressed her lips together, waiting for an answer.

CHAPTER 7

WAY OF THE WILD

"I'm sure he meant no harm, Miss Perlmutter," Mr. McWaid tried to explain his son's actions. "It's just that Patrick and his brother have quite active imaginations, you see. They imagine things, after all, as boys often do."

"It takes no imagination." Miss Perlmutter stepped over to her trunk, took out a long-bladed knife, and quickly pried open the top of the barrel next to the one Patrick had just searched. At first it looked like all the other barrels, filled with rough grains of wheat. But as Patrick and his father watched, she reached in and grabbed the handle of a hefty military-style rifle, pulled it straight up, and lifted it out slowly for all to see.

"Is this vhat you saw?" she asked. She dusted the weapon off and tossed it casually to Mr. McWaid. "This one is not loaded, except vith grain. Only one I keep ready."

"B-but . . ." It was Mr. McWaid's turn to stutter. He nearly dropped the rifle, which to Patrick looked very odd in his father's hands.

"Five others," she explained, pointing out one of the other barrels, "in that one there. And a dozen other tools, as vell. Picks and shovels. Some dynamite."

"Dynamite!" Mr. McWaid whistled.

"So I really *did* see a gun!" Patrick couldn't take his eyes off the rifle. Even with all the grain dust, it looked like a serious weapon. On the side, near the trigger, he could read the initials *CSA*.

"I am certainly no firearms expert," continued Miss Perlmutter. "But the man who sold these to me said they vere from America. Confederate army supplies, left over from their Civil War."

"But why are you hiding them like some kind of smuggler?" Mr. McWaid gently handed back the rifle. Patrick could remember seeing a man handle a wet baby in the same way.

"Thieves, of course," replied Miss Perlmutter matter-of-factly. She buried the wicked-looking weapon back in the barrel. "These tools are for the colony." She looked at them once again, then all the way around them to see if anyone else was close-by. "Ach, vell, I'll tell you the entire story, but you must promise not to tell anyone."

"If you're breaking any laws, Miss . . ." Mr. McWaid held up his finger in warning. "We've already been through enough of that with other passengers. You, on the other hand, were the last one I'd have suspected."

"Ach, no." Miss Perlmutter waved him off like a fly. "It's nothing illegal. I hide them for safekeeping, that's all."

"But for whom?" Patrick wondered.

"The men at the colony need the tools. One has discovered . . ." She paused. "One of the men has discovered copper on our property. Ve intend to dig a small mine. I vas sent to bring back these tools. Qvietly, you know?"

"You?" Patrick still couldn't believe it.

"Perhaps they thought no one vould suspect an old German voman like me."

Finally Mr. McWaid nodded. "I see."

"Ja, but no one else must know. You must promise."

"Your secret is safe with us, Miss Perlmutter. Is it not, Patrick?"

Patrick nodded, too, just as Firestorm came up behind him. The dog first sniffed, then took another step forward and growled at Miss Perlmutter's thick, black-stockinged ankles.

"But the dog still doesn't like me, I see." The slightest hint of a smile crossed Miss Perlmutter's face.

"Pa!" bawled Michael. Patrick heard his brother stumble down the deck, knock over a crate, and slide breathlessly to their feet.

"Slow down there, boy." Patrick's father turned and held out his hand to stop Michael from falling on his face. "There's no need to hurry so."

"But, Pa." Michael's face was streaked with tears, and his chest was heaving with sobs. "He's gone. He's really gone!"

"Who are you talking about, Michael?" Mr. McWaid tried to calm his son down with his hands on Michael's heaving shoulders. "Who's gone?"

"I think he's talking about Christopher, Pa," Patrick answered as Michael tried to keep from sobbing. He grabbed his brother's hand and marched him away from Miss Perlmutter's hideout. "Come on, Michael, stop that and show me where you saw him last."

In a few minutes the whole family was searching the paddle steamer, calling and whistling.

"Christopher!" hollered Becky as they looked in all the places the koala was used to hiding in: under boxes, up in the wheelhouse, even under the covers of the bed in the captain's state-room.

"Where *is* he?" wondered Patrick, checking for the third time under the galley table. "We've looked everywhere."

"Not everyvhere," declared Miss Perlmutter. "Ve still haven't found the one place vhere your bear is."

Which was true, but it didn't seem to make Michael feel any better. Not until he finally looked up to see the furry koala clinging to the top of the paddle steamer's own crane.

"There!" Michael pointed up excitedly. "You come down from there, Christopher! That's not a eucalyptus tree for you to climb in!"

"Don't you think your animal vould be happier in the vild?" asked Miss Perlmutter as they ate their supper late that evening. Michael stuffed his mouth full of boiled beets, probably so he wouldn't have to answer the question.

I know how you feel, thought Patrick, and the German woman pointed at Michael's face with her fork.

"Vhat if the animal had scratched you in the eye," she asked, "instead of just the cheek? You know, Gott gave you only two eyes, young man."

Mrs. McWaid frowned and looked more closely at Michael's face.

"Christopher's never done anything like that before," put in Patrick before his mother could say anything. Michael nodded his support. "He's always been so shy and gentle. Michael's raised Christopher since he was tiny. It was an accident."

"Perhaps." Miss Perlmutter looked outside at the grove of trees that hung out over the river, just beyond the Mannum wharf. "But your tiny koala is qvite grown-up now."

Qvite grown-up, thought Patrick. He knew exactly what she was saying, even with her accent.

"And if you ask me," she went on, "the poor animal belongs out there."

Michael chewed and chewed. Tears filled his eyes.

"What do you say, Michael?" wondered their father. "You have to admit, the little beast doesn't take to handling the way he used to. And you've noticed in the last few weeks how he's always looking for ways to wander off. Don't you think he would be happier out in the bush with other koalas? He's old enough now to make it on his own."

"No!" Michael scraped his chair backward and stood up. Firestorm jumped out of the way; he'd been prospecting the floor for handouts. "We're the ones who take care of him. We saved his life. He belongs with us!"

"Come on, Michael," said Becky. "Perhaps Miss Perlmutter is right."

"No, no, NO!"

Michael ran from the salon, his hands pressed to his ears. No one got up to follow him.

"Oh dear." Mrs. McWaid looked across the table at her husband.

"Perhaps I never should have let him take that animal in. Look at the heartbreak it's caused."

Miss Perlmutter put up her hand. "The problem vill solve itself vhen this koala disappears on his own. It von't be long."

"You think so?" wondered Mrs. McWaid.

"Ja, absolute. It's a vild animal, you know. He'll move on, find his own vay to the vild."

"Just like Jeff." The words slipped out of Patrick's mouth before he even thought of saying them. He practically bit his tongue, but it was too late.

"Pardon me?" asked Miss Perlmutter. "Jeff?"

Becky had heard him, though. She dropped her napkin on her plate and rushed away from the table. Patrick's mother gave him a stern look.

"You didn't need to remind your sister like that," she said. "You know how much she misses Jefferson. It's not just you."

"By the way," said Mr. McWaid, "we passed the *Victoria* this afternoon. Did anyone else notice?"

Patrick hadn't. And his mother's words rang in Patrick's ears when he finally wandered outside after dinner to see what Michael was doing on deck. He wiggled his shoulders in the chill, but he didn't mind the dark.

"He's going to scratch you again, Michael," Patrick warned him. "And you'd better put him down, or he's going to fall right over the side of the boat."

"He would never leave us, would he, Patrick?"

Patrick didn't want to answer.

"Don't you think, Patrick?"

"Miss Perlmutter thinks so."

Michael held tighter to the koala, and he tried to keep his head away from the long, sharp claws that had already scratched him once in the face. Christopher squirmed and kept staring at the blue gum trees across the river from where they were tied up.

"Anyway," continued Michael, "have you seen the big ostrich recently?"

"Why, what's wrong with him?"

"Maybe he's all right now. But take a look when you feed them tonight. It's the one that escaped. He isn't standing up."

Sure enough, when Patrick went to feed the ostriches later, he noticed the biggest bird slumped in the corner of its cage. Patrick poured some coarse grain into the metal bowl built into the side of the crate and shook it around. The other birds discovered the treat in an instant.

"Come on, you." Patrick reached around and poked at the third ostrich, but it hardly looked back at him. And it certainly didn't attack his arm, the way it had done to Michael just that morning.

"You have to eat, big fellow. Or at least stand up. Something. Anything."

The other two in the cage paused from the meal long enough to look down at the sick ostrich as if wondering what was wrong. Patrick poked and prodded, but the ill bird only closed its eyes.

"Please?" He stroked its feathers and wished he knew what to do. He prayed silently for the bird, and then he even thought about praying for Jefferson to come back, but changed his mind.

God? he prayed. *Hello?*

He heard a shuffling behind him and looked back to see Miss Perlmutter standing in the shadows, watching with sad eyes. He wasn't sure how long she had been there.

"Perhaps your bird vill be feeling better in the morning," she told him.

Locust Plague

But the ostrich *wasn't* better in the morning. And it wasn't better the next day, or the next. In fact . . .

"You mustn't blame yourself," his father told him, feeding another piece of wood into the steam boiler. "You fed it and took care of it just fine. You did a fine job. There was nothing else you could do."

The flames licked out the door of the boiler and curled back the hair on Mr. McWaid's hand. Inside the engine, steam began to fizzle and pop. But they were already late that morning. They had to be on their way.

"There must have been something more." Patrick wanted to kick something. "There must have been something else I could do, besides just . . . just stand there and watch him die. Maybe I should have prayed more."

"It wasn't just you." Patrick's father put a hand on his shoulder. "We were all here, remember? I couldn't do anything. Your mother couldn't do anything. Even Miss Perlmutter had no idea what to do. It was just one of those things you're going to have to accept from God. Part of growing up."

Patrick wished his father hadn't added that last part—the part about growing up. Between Jeff and Miss Perlmutter, he'd heard just about all he'd wanted to hear on the subject.

"Maybe he just couldn't stand being in the cage anymore," suggested Michael. "Or maybe it was because he didn't like you riding him."

"Michael!" Mr. McWaid scolded. "That's not it, and you know it. If it had anything to do with being in a cage, I'm sure it would have happened already during the rough ride over from Africa. It was nothing of Patrick's doing, you can be sure of it."

Patrick wasn't so sure. Time after time he kept replaying the past few days in his mind. The ostrich not eating, not getting up, and finally just closing its eyes.

Maybe if I had . . . But he didn't know what else he could have done. Maybe his father was right. What he really wanted was to curl up in a warm bed and not wake up for ten years. Not until he was *really* grown-up.

"Pa!" came Becky's voice from outside. Their father slammed the boiler door shut, clapped his hands, and straightened out.

"Pa, I think you should come out here," said Becky, and her voice sounded a notch higher from excitement. Or was it worry? One or the other.

"What is it, Becky?" Mr. McWaid checked one of the steam gauges for pressure. "I'm right in the middle of firing up here. Can it wait?"

"I don't think so." This time there was no mistaking the panic in Becky's voice. "I've never seen anything like this."

Becky was right. And once they were under way, they stared for hour after hour as thick clouds of locusts washed over them. Sometimes they could hardly see the shore, only yards away, as Becky held their course up the river.

"Where did they all come from?" wondered Patrick, flicking another locust off his arm.

"The same place they came from in the plagues of Moses," pronounced Miss Perlmutter. She had climbed up to the enclosed pilothouse to watch with them. "From the hand of Gott. Only now the locusts are coming farther south." She pointed at the swarms that darkened the sun overhead. "This is vhat ate our German colony's gardens, you know."

"And that's why your people need the grain we're bringing," added Becky through clenched teeth. "I wish we could go faster."

"Don't vorry yourself." Miss Perlmutter patted Becky's hand. "You don't vant to be vorrying about things you cannot change, the vay your brother does. Vorry ist a sin, you know. Ve're going as fast as we can. I know that. You know that, too, don't you?"

Patrick pretended not to hear as the German woman swatted calmly at the insects with a rolled-up paper. Even with the door closed, the locusts somehow found their way into the pilothouse, bouncing like springs underfoot. Every few minutes Patrick had to open the door, lean out, and sweep them from the window with a broom so Becky could see to steer.

"Well, at least *someone* is enjoying this." Mr. McWaid stepped inside, slammed the door behind him, and waved back another swarm. "Looks like your ostriches are having a jolly feast, Patrick."

"Can they get sick?" Patrick was still thinking about the ostrich that had died.

Mr. McWaid shook his head no. "Good for them, I imagine. Gives them some variety in their diet."

"In fact," said Miss Perlmutter, warming up to the subject, "many tribal people in Africa and South America eat nothing *but* insects. Locusts are qvite good for you. And vhat about John the Baptist? He ate locusts, ja?"

"We're not tribal people." Patrick wrinkled his nose and shivered at the thought. "And didn't John the Baptist have honey to choke them down with?"

After a long day of swatting locusts, Patrick was very sure he didn't want to see the bugs on a plate. Even more sure that he would never, ever, eat one. Not if his life depended on it.

"P-too!" He wiped his lips after yet another locust flew at his mouth. The locusts, it seemed, were doing their best to offer him a taste. He spit one more out into the darkening evening.

"Getting hard to see," said Mr. McWaid. He pointed to a bend in the river, off to the right. "Let's stop here before we run into something."

He vaulted down the ladder to slow the engine while Patrick

readied their mooring lines. Just as they had for the past few days, they would tie up to the biggest trees they could find, front and rear, and get a few hours sleep before hurrying on early the next morning.

"Closer . . ." yelled Patrick, waving at his sister to steer more to the right. "Just a little more." He could see more water between them and the shore, and a few dark trees. With the mooring rope in his hand, he stood ready to leap to shore. Four feet, three feet . . .

Patrick was in midair before he realized that the tree he was jumping toward was not a tree. That is, not unless the tree had dark, shining eyes and white teeth that glittered in the soft light from the *Lady Elisabeth*'s lanterns.

"What. . . ?" Patrick would have turned in midair if he could have. Instead, he crashed into the chest of a tall aborigine man, sending them both tumbling to the spongy ground between two overhanging trees. In turn they bowled over a couple of others behind the first man. The two of them tangled in the rope from the paddle steamer, with Patrick pinned under the man's considerable weight.

He couldn't move; he could hardly breathe. And he certainly couldn't yell for help.

But Patrick was glad he didn't need to; as he lay gasping like a fish in the bottom of a fishing boat, someone else jumped over to untangle them.

"Pa?" Patrick managed to groan. He supposed the aborigine fellow had also had the air knocked out of him. He wasn't sure what had happened to the other people behind him, though.

"Up now, *mein Freund*!" commanded Miss Perlmutter, for there was no mistaking the voice. First she took the tall man by the arms and lifted him out of the tangled nest of rope. He rocked for a moment as Patrick lay on his back, gasping for breath. The man still reminded Patrick of a large tree, he was so tall. At least a head taller than Miss Perlmutter, and she was one of the tallest women Patrick had ever met. She was also one of the fastest women, when she wanted to be. Patrick couldn't imagine how she had followed him to shore so quickly.

When the aborigine fellow saw Miss Perlmutter in her sensible black dress, he nearly fell over again from surprise.

"Miss P . . ." And that was all Patrick could manage to say. He reached out his hand, and she pulled him up, as well. His shoulder felt as if it might pop out of its socket.

"There, there," she told him, picking up the rope. "You're all right. But I think you'd better look before you leap, young man. Don't you?"

"Yes, ma'am."

The steam engine shut down with a cough and a whimper, and in a moment Mr. McWaid was up on deck holding a small lantern.

"Secure up front, Patrick?" he asked, then gave a little gasp. "Oh, Miss Perlmutter, I didn't realize . . ."

"Ve have a couple of dinner guests," she announced, pulling on the collar of the aborigine man's old plaid shirt. There was no telling where he had gotten it, though the shirt matched the faded black trousers for being dirty and ragged. In any case, he had no choice but to follow Miss Perlmutter aboard the *Lady E*.

"Your friends, too!" barked the woman, and again there was no arguing with her. Even if they didn't speak her language, as the tall man obviously didn't, they obeyed instantly, without protest.

"Patrick," called Becky from the wheelhouse. "Are you all right? I could see what was happening, but I couldn't stop you."

Patrick took a slow breath and looped the end of his rope around the trunk of a sturdy-looking eucalyptus.

"I just had the wind knocked out of me," he squeaked. He still didn't have enough breath to answer very loudly. All he knew was that it was going to be an interesting dinner.

"Vhat?" asked Miss Perlmutter, sitting up straighter in her chair. "Are you not pleased to share a meal vith these people?"

She sounded shocked at the very idea.

"After all," she continued, "these are men and vomen for whom our Lord died, is that not right? I vould have thought—"

"Of course they are, Miss Perlmutter." Mr. McWaid tried to smile, but it came out looking a little forced. "It's just that . . . well, we weren't prepared for quite so many visitors."

Their guest of honor sat at the end of the table, sampling Mrs. McWaid's Irish stew, mixing in locusts like salt and pepper and smiling with delight. Four of his friends sat nearby, leaving hardly any room at the table for anyone else. Michael had been excused early to help clean up.

"John," warned Mrs. McWaid, "you must remember to be hospitable. Perhaps they understand some of what we're saying."

The aborigine nodded and smiled. He seemed about the same age as Patrick's parents. But Patrick had a hard time telling exactly.

And as the man continued to dip wriggling insect delicacies into the stew, Patrick put a hand to his forehead and tried not to look. His stomach turned at the crunching sound.

"He wants you to try one," whispered Becky.

And sure enough, the big man held out a locust for Patrick to try. He insisted.

CHAPTER 9

MISS P'S DEFENSE

"No, no, no," answered Patrick, closing his eyes and holding up his hands. "Believe me, you don't want to see me get sick."

Finally the man gave up, and the adults continued the conversation.

"The locals don't seem to be disturbed at all with the locusts," observed Mr. McWaid. A few more of the pests had managed to slip in the salon the last time someone opened the side door.

"Qvite the contrary," said Miss Perlmutter. "They're enjoying them almost as much as the ostriches are."

"And speaking of ostriches," reported Becky. "Did you know that Michael has a lantern and is showing the birds to three or four of this fellow's friends? Isn't he supposed to be helping with the dishes?"

Mrs. McWaid sighed and looked at her husband, who shrugged his *What can I do?* look.

"Patrick, go check on your brother, would you, please?" Mr. McWaid requested. "Remind him he has chores to do."

Without looking, Patrick wolfed another bite of his mother's stew. He instantly regretted it as his teeth sank into something crunchy and juicy. His throat clamped shut. Tighter than if someone were strangling him. Slowly he peeked down at his bowl to see another small locust swimming in the sauce, halfway between a chunk of beef and a carrot.

"Excuse me," he mumbled through a mouthful of stew. He knew what he had to do, and he had only a second or two to make it through the door and out to the deck railing. . . .

Patrick rolled over and over on his sleeping mat later that night. On his side, on his back, again on his side . . . It didn't matter much. His stomach still turned when he thought about biting into the locust. A couple more had crawled up on his blanket, and he could barely see them in the dim moonlight streaming through the window.

"Shoo!" He sent the insects flying with a kick of his toe. He could hear Miss Perlmutter snoring out on the deck.

"Hear that, Michael?" he whispered. Michael didn't answer, so Patrick just lay there listening to the boat and wind sounds and the whispering of the leaves on the trees. The river's music. He didn't hear it much during the day, when the steam engine and the paddle wheels drowned out just about everything else. But at night . . .

And then he heard something else. Very slight it was, like someone holding his breath and then letting it out again. The sound of the waves and the boat's gentle rocking changed for just an instant. But Patrick knew.

Someone just stepped on board, he told himself.

He raised up on one elbow to listen, but all he could hear was snoring—his father's on the inside, Miss Perlmutter's on the outside.

Had he imagined it?

No, Patrick decided as he slipped out from under his blanket. He was afraid to stand up, though, afraid to look out the windows.

What if they see me? He wondered who might be sneaking around on their paddle steamer at this time of night. Midnight, was it? Maybe. Dark, anyway.

He smashed a couple of locusts with his knees as he crawled

past the galley to the side door. Surely whoever had come aboard wouldn't dare come inside, would they? He crouched by the side door in his underwear, shivering, wondering, listening.

A moment later he jumped to hear the squeak of a rusty door hinge opening, outside on deck.

It's close, he decided. Patrick straightened up oh-so-slowly, finally enough to see out the window. He saw nothing, only the dark shapes and shadows of all the cargo crowded on deck.

For a moment he thought about waking his father, but he worried what Pa would say if it was nothing. Nothing? There was the rustling sound again, and it sounded as if it was coming from somewhere around the bird crates. He hurried back to his bed and slipped on his trousers and shirt without a sound. What would he do if he met up with something—or someone—out in the shadows?

Silly, he told himself, trying to forget the nagging feeling that someone was snooping around outside. *It's just the ostriches. That's all.*

After retracing his steps, he slowly pushed open the door and tiptoed out onto the deck. He winced at the feeling of crushed locusts under his bare toes and tried to lift his feet higher. As if that would help.

And then he was sure of it. The birds rustled, but there was something else, too. He knocked his shin into a crate in the dark and almost cried out, but he bit his tongue instead.

Someone is out here!

A grunt, and one of the birds rustled its feathers. Miss Perlmutter stopped snoring. Patrick's mouth felt dry.

"Hello?" he whispered and stepped around the corner to where he could see the ostrich crates, on the side of the boat nearest shore. The two men froze at the sound of Patrick's voice. One stood in the moonlight behind an ostrich, and the other had a short length of rope around the bird's neck. Both men wore pants only, no shoes, no shirts. Another step and they'd have their catch off the boat and into the bush—only, the bird wasn't exactly cooperating.

"What are you doing?" squeaked Patrick, but of course it was obvious.

The two aborigines stared at Patrick. Even in the dark, he was pretty sure they were two of the men who had been on the boat earlier that evening—out on the deck, not the ones who had eaten with them. One of them grinned at him, a big toothy grin, and Patrick remembered seeing him before. But they didn't stop what they were doing.

"Wait." Patrick couldn't believe what he was seeing. He stepped toward the men and grabbed hold of the dangling rope. "You can't do this."

But they could and they were, and they were obviously much stronger than Patrick in the tug-of-war that followed. For a moment it went back and forth, but with one strong shove Patrick went flying backward, crashing into a couple of Miss Perlmutter's grain barrels.

"Oh!" Patrick knocked the back of his head, slumped against the barrels, and slid to the deck. For a moment the deck below shifted and swirled. The man pulling the ostrich shrieked in laughter, and the other joined in. It surely wasn't quiet anymore. The rest of his family must have heard what was happening.

"That vill be qvite enough." Miss Perlmutter's take-charge voice had never sounded so good as she stepped out of the shadows behind him.

Even so, the two ostrich thieves paid as much attention to her as they had to Patrick. That is, until they heard a distinctive *click*.

"Halten Sie!" She had switched over to a high-pitched German. That got their attention. One of the men pointed to the Confederate rifle she gripped in her hands, just before the ear-splitting explosion.

"Miss P!" shouted Patrick, shielding his face with his arms.

"Ayee!" shrieked one of the thieves. He flew over his partner in crime, scrambling and tumbling for cover. And in a wild, panicked moment, they disappeared from sight, crashing through the bush. Patrick guessed they wouldn't be back soon.

Stranger still was the sight of Miss Perlmutter. Patrick stared at the woman in her flowered flannel nightgown, holding her smoking rifle pointed straight in the air. Her face was as pale as the half-moon above, her expression stricken—as if she had actually shot someone instead of just shooting up into the air.

"Are you all right, Miss Perlmutter?" Patrick got to his feet, rubbing the back of his head. A few stars still twinkled in front of his eyes, and they were not stars in the sky.

Miss Perlmutter didn't answer but just stared off into the night. Her hands trembled.

"Whatever is happening out here?" bellowed Mr. McWaid. Wrapped in a flannel blanket, he burst through the side door and tumbled onto the deck. Mrs. McWaid and Michael were right behind him, adding to the confusion. Finally Becky came out with a lantern.

"Patrick?" Mrs. McWaid grabbed her son.

"Miss Perlmutter?" Becky rushed to the woman's side and held the lantern high.

"Look at the ostrich. He's frozen!" exclaimed Michael.

Patrick grabbed the rope around the bird's neck, but there was no hurry. The ostrich hadn't moved from his spot on the deck where the two men left him. He was shaking as much as Miss Perlmutter.

"I am sorry." Miss Perlmutter finally lowered the weapon and handed it to Patrick's father. "I am terribly sorry. I did not mean to startle anyone."

For a moment Mr. McWaid studied the smoking gun. Then he lowered his head, and his shoulders started to shake.

CHAPTER 10

SHIP IN THE NIGHT

"What's wrong, dear?" wondered Mrs. McWaid, looking at her husband. A smoking gun, an upset Miss Perlmutter, and now this . . .

"Nothing." His snorts turned into chuckles. "Absolutely nothing. She says she didn't mean to startle anyone. Did you hear her say that?"

Michael was the first to join in, and his giggles soon caught on with Patrick, then Becky. Their mother held a hand in front of her mouth, hiding a grin, even as she waved at her husband to stop.

But it was far too late for that. The more they laughed, the harder it was to stop and the more confused a red-faced Miss Perlmutter became.

"Certainly you do not find this incident amusing," she sputtered, looking from face to face. "I am ashamed. These men, perhaps they vere hungry. I should have offered them something to eat. Perhaps it vas not the Christian thing to do, firing a dangerous veapon. It vas not funny."

"No, of course not." Mr. McWaid laughed until the tears streamed down his cheeks. "Seeing you out here in your nightgown holding that silly old rifle, scaring away ostrich thieves, is very serious. This is certainly . . . not . . . funny."

"Not funny at all," agreed Mrs. McWaid, holding her sides.

"You should have seen the look on their faces, though," gasped Patrick between breaths. "When the one fellow noticed what she was holding in her hands, he crawled up his partner's back as if it were a ladder."

"A ladder," echoed Michael, which sent them all into a new gale of laughter. And hearing his sister's delicate "he-he-he" only made Patrick laugh even more—if that was possible. Michael rolled on the deck.

"Oh dear." Mrs. McWaid finally wiped her eyes and squared her shoulders. "We really mustn't. You can see it's distressing the poor woman."

"You may give orders like a Prussian field marshal," said Mr. McWaid, "but I think perhaps you're not as tough as you appear to be."

Mr. McWaid quickly checked the rifle and held it out to Miss Perlmutter, but she held her palms out to stop him.

"Nein," she said. "I have done enough damage for one night. Never again. I vas only trying to protect the boy. I . . . did not think enough."

Her words brought the chuckles to an end, and they all stared at the weeping woman. She dabbed at her eyes with the sleeve of her nightgown. Hers were not tears of laughter.

"Thank you, Miss P," said Patrick, at once serious. "I don't think the aborigines would have hurt me. They were probably just taking the bird back to their camp for food. But thank you."

Miss Perlmutter nodded and backed away from the odd scene, then whispered something to Mrs. McWaid. Patrick led the still-trembling ostrich back to its cage. Then they all headed for bed.

"Are you going to be all right, Patrick?" asked his mother. "Miss Perlmutter tells me you bumped your head when those fellows pushed you."

"It was nothing," replied Patrick, and he meant it. He and Michael found their sleeping mats again in the salon. "Let's get some sleep."

Michael made a rustling sound, as if he was burrowing under his sheets, while Patrick lay as still as he could, listening for the aborigine men to return. But a half hour passed and nothing happened. He listened to Michael's heavy breathing, then the gentle lullaby water sounds that usually put him to sleep. And after a while, the distant *wooo* of a steam whistle.

A steam whistle? At this time of night? He wondered who would be out on the river, risking an accident. Whichever paddle steamer it was, they were obviously in a very big hurry.

A half hour later he heard it again, only closer.

Well, I can't sleep anyway, he decided, pushing back his blanket one more time and sitting up. He wondered who else would be awake as the approaching paddle steamer's bright lights glowed in the distance, through the trees, like a moving sunrise. Michael didn't move, but he had to be awake. It was like a train passing, all the hissing and splashing and shouting.

And bright, too. Probably had a full set of expensive new lanterns, enough to turn the night to day. So maybe the paddle steamer ran all day and all night, with a couple of crews. Some of the bigger paddle steamers did that, Patrick knew.

Patrick saw it coming, but still he blinked at the army of light that suddenly threw crisp shadows across the walls. He counted at least four big searchlights mounted on the front and upper decks of the boat.

And for such a big thing, the boat moved fast. Patrick wondered how it ever fit in the narrow river. They probably wouldn't notice the *Lady Elisabeth* tucked away in a gentle backwater under the trees. But Patrick had no trouble making out the name on the front railing of the passerby.

"The *Victoria,*" he gasped. Not that it should have been such a surprise. Mr. McWaid had already told them the fancy paddle steamer had been stopped farther down the river a few days back. Now it was the *Victoria*'s turn to leapfrog ahead of the *Lady E.*

A few men were out on deck, enjoying the night air, maybe, or watching the river ahead for dangerous logs. One man was singing a river song, and the words floated over the water. Something about being "out on the angry sea," and how they would go "rapping the cooks' back doors on the *Murrumbidgee.*"

Patrick tried to focus on the men as they passed by. He noticed one in the background, away from the others. *Jefferson.*

Without realizing it, Patrick raised his hand to wave to his old friend. He caught himself, and even in the darkness he felt silly. Of course Jefferson couldn't see him as the giant riverboat passed by. The American did lean on the railing and stare in their direction, but Patrick was pretty sure that all Jeff could see were the dark trees and riverbank shadows.

But was Jeff all right? He hadn't seemed himself at all back in Goolwa.

"See you again, Jeff." Patrick wasn't sure when he would—if ever. He flopped back down and buried his face in his pillow. A minute later all he felt were a few locusts crawling on his blanket and the lapping waves left behind by the passing *Victoria*. The waves rocked him to a fitful sleep.

The big paddle steamer looked different in the late afternoon light. Bigger, even, if that was possible. Patrick frowned as they caught up with the *Victoria*. It had been less than a day since the other riverboat had passed them in the night.

"Pa," Patrick asked quietly. "Are we going to stop here, too?"

Mr. McWaid leaned over Becky's shoulder and pointed with his finger for her to turn the wheel a bit more to the right. That would take them closer to where the other paddle steamer had pulled up to the bank.

"Plenty of room for two boats to tie up here, son. And we need the wood."

Patrick nodded. Of course they had no choice but to stop at Emu Flat. They had stopped at the quiet wood station before. A hollow-cheeked man lived there in a tiny bark hut with his round little wife and a red-eyed baby that screamed most of the time.

Emu flat? Patrick had never seen any emus there. But he knew the big Australian birds had lived there. Pa told him that emus were scared off into the bush years ago when rowdy paddle steamer crews first began stopping there for wood.

And the wood! Patrick had always wondered how the frail man could chop and split so much. There it was, though, stacked in neat bundles on the shore—enormous amounts of firewood for the unending appetites of the river's paddle steamers.

"I just hope they leave some for us," murmured Patrick. He watched some of the *Victoria*'s deckhands carry armloads of firewood back and forth.

"Ah, but aren't you the worrier." Mr. McWaid moved for the door. "Isn't this the vessel our friend Jeff is on? Thought you'd want to see him."

Patrick nodded and turned away.

Out on the forward deck, Michael was wrestling with Christopher. Once again it looked as if Christopher was winning.

"You stay still," Michael commanded the squirming koala. "And stop scratching me. When we tie up, I'll be sure to get you some fresh leaves. That's what's wrong, eh? You're hungry, that's all. Now, just wait a minute."

They had slowed way down and were coasting into place beside the much larger paddle steamer. Becky had quickly become an expert at maneuvering their boat in and out of tight spots. Their father had said she had "just the right touch."

Michael, on the other hand, was still having a hard time. First he tried to hold Christopher tightly, then at arm's length, then . . .

"You'd better let him go," Patrick told him sourly. "Can't you see he doesn't want to be held?"

"Yes, he does. He's just—OUCH!"

Christopher's claws must have connected with Michael's arm just then, because Michael had to let go. Problem was, they were standing too close to the edge. Patrick heard the cry before the splash.

"Man overboard!" hollered Michael, jumping up and down and waving his hands at Becky. "I mean, koala overboard! Stop! We're going to run him over!"

Becky swung the wheel away, but they were drifting too slowly to change course very quickly. She shook her head helplessly and held her grip on the wheel.

Patrick checked down at the dark river where the churning ball of wet fur was trying to keep his head above water. He was caught in a canyon between the two paddle steamers, and the walls were closing in.

"We've got to do something!" yelled Michael, pacing the deck wildly above the spot where Christopher was struggling to stay afloat. He started to kick off his shoes, but Patrick held him back.

CHAPTER 11

DANGER AT THE BILLABONG

"You can't go in after him," warned Patrick. "He'll slice you up with those claws. Or the boats will squash you."

For a moment the thought of the koala crushed between the boats made Patrick panic. But there seemed to be nothing to do but watch helplessly. Then he felt a pole poke him in the back.

"Move aside there," barked Miss Perlmutter, "and grab this pole."

Patrick did as told before he realized what they were holding. Miss Perlmutter had stretched a large frilly cloth between two long rake handles. It looked like a scarecrow in . . . a petticoat?

"Now, keep the net tight," ordered Miss Perlmutter. She gripped a rake handle under her arm. "You have a pole, and I have the other pole. And ve shcoop the animal up qvickly, like a fish."

Actually, Miss Perlmutter's invention reminded Patrick of giant chopsticks, only with the "net" stretched over the pointed-down end. And it *was* a frilly petticoat. One of the ends began to rip as Patrick held his pole tight.

"Oh, I'm sorry," began Patrick, but the German woman had no time for small talk. She grunted back and pointed with her nose.

"Underneath the little beast now" she said. *"Eins, zwei, drei!"*

Patrick knew she was counting to three by the way she said it, and he reached down with her to scoop Christopher up in one swift move. They would have him safely on deck in a moment.

"Got him!" yelled Michael, loudly enough for everyone to hear. They were almost close enough to the other paddle steamer to jump across to its other deck.

"You're wonderful, Miss Perlmutter!" Michael jumped up and down with a huge smile on his face, then bent down to make sure his pet was all right. Miss Perlmutter nodded just slightly and grinned.

Until she heard the whistling and clapping from the *Victoria*.

"Nice petticoat, Grandma!" yelled one of the crew, and they all laughed. Miss Perlmutter turned beet red and gathered up the dripping clothes.

"How about catching us some fish with that net?" called another. That was all Patrick could take.

"How about keeping your big mouth shut?" Patrick yelled back, and he felt the temper inside him snap like a trap. "That's not the way you speak to a lady."

"That's right," Michael chimed in. "You can't talk to Miss Perlmutter like that."

"Let me handle this, Michael," Patrick whispered and held his brother back, but Michael ignored him. At least three tall uniformed deckhands grinned over at them, but just then it didn't matter to Patrick.

"Oh, we've got a feisty one, have we?" said the biggest one. Miss Perlmutter whirled to face him across the gap between the two boats.

"Come pay us a visit, Red." The man in the middle sneered at Patrick and motioned with his hand. "Bring your granny with you, and we'll teach you some respect."

"You should be ashamed of yourselves," sputtered Miss Perlmutter. "Have you nothing better to do than bother little boys? Vhat's your name, young man?"

Patrick wondered what the debate would have been like without the river between them. The big sailor laughed and scratched his nose.

"And who wants to know?"

Out of the corner of his eye, Patrick caught a small movement, a tiny flash of blue uniform. He looked up higher to see the *Victoria*'s First Officer York, standing watch over them from his perch high up on the third deck, just outside the wheelhouse. A wicked smile instantly disappeared from the man's face, replaced by a serious scowl, as he straightened up. But too late—Patrick had seen it.

"You three!" bellowed York's loud voice. "Make yourselves useful. There's still wood that needs stacking before we get out of this stinking billabong."

"Yes, sir, Officer York." The big man deflated, and his shoulders dropped. He trapped a locust in his hand and flicked it across the water at them. The other two deckhands snapped to attention as if they had heard a voice from heaven itself.

"We'll see you later, boy," whispered the man, and Patrick had to turn away. "Maybe you need to learn more respect."

Patrick understood the threat completely, even if he didn't understand what he had done to deserve it. And where was Jefferson all this time?

"Wait for me!" For a moment Patrick panicked when he lost sight of his sister on the way to the woodpile. He thought the sailors were all back at the *Victoria*, but he wasn't sure.

"Oh!" He bumped into Becky in the dark.

"Watch out, Patrick," she gently scolded.

"I am. Do you see them anywhere?"

"Last I saw they were still back on the *Victoria*." She knew what he was talking about. If Patrick had been a few years younger, he would have held his older sister's hand. His feet made sucking sounds as they followed the muddy path to the rest of the woodpiles, hidden back in the bush. The tough sailors of the *Victoria* had claimed all the best wood, closer to the shore. He wished he could still see the cheery lantern light inside the *Lady Elisabeth*, back behind them.

"I think this should be the last trip, don't you?" Becky asked him. Patrick thought she sounded as hopeful as he felt.

"We'll *make* it the last trip."

Patrick stumbled and tried to remember how many times they had walked back and forth along the trail. He'd lost count somewhere around twenty-five or twenty-six. Becky might have been small, yes, but she could sure tote her share of firewood.

"I still don't understand why Jeff hasn't talked to us," mumbled Patrick.

"I think it's that awful Officer York." Becky didn't sound very encouraging. "Every time I see Jeff out on the deck, York yells at him and tells him to do more work."

"Becky!" called Mrs. McWaid from the paddle steamer. Her voice floated out over the early evening air, though they couldn't see her through the dark and the trees. "We're having dinner soon. You and the boys clean up now."

Patrick looked at Becky, and he could barely see the expression on her face. Some light from the moon helped, but not much.

"You mean Patrick?" Becky called back. "Michael isn't with us."

"I thought Michael was helping Miss Perlmutter," Patrick told his sister. "Back on the boat."

She nodded.

"Michael's not here, Ma," Becky called back, trotting closer to the shore, where they could faintly see the *Lady E* and their mother. Patrick followed his sister. "Patrick and I haven't see him for the past half hour."

"Oh, that Michael." Mrs. McWaid stood at the edge of the deck with her hands on her hips. "He said he was going to gather some leaves for that confounded koala bear, and your father told him to be sure to stay with you two. I think he took the dog along. You really haven't seen him?"

Patrick couldn't remember when his mother had called the koala "confounded" before, but he was sure she meant it.

"We'll find him, Ma," Patrick replied. "I'm sure he can't be far."

"Please stay together!"

That would not be a problem, thought Patrick, and he shivered at the sound of men laughing on the *Victoria*. A card game, maybe. Was Jefferson playing? He didn't think so. Probably mopping the floors for everyone.

"Michael?" called Becky, looking toward a shadowy grove of trees.

"He can't be far," said Patrick, wanting to believe what he was saying. "Not if he's just looking for leaves for Christopher."

"He's always doing this!" Becky picked a handful of fallen eucalyptus leaves and tossed them impatiently into the air. "He just wanders off without even thinking of how he's going to worry Ma and Pa."

"Michael!" Patrick called out toward another grove of trees. "Firestorm!" He picked his way more carefully down the path, feeling for the soft spots.

"Careful," he warned Becky. "I saw a couple of billabongs back here. Really marshy, where we could just sink into the water. Maybe Michael . . ."

Patrick didn't finish the sentence but pressed on faster. *Maybe Michael stepped right into a billabong in the dark and drowned.*

"If we don't find him in two minutes," said Becky, her voice shaking just a bit, "we're going back to get help."

Patrick nodded and shivered. The trees rustled overhead and a bird called as they wandered farther into the bush. A few of the bushes lashed at his legs. Just a little farther.

Where is *he?* wondered Patrick. Michael always had a way of wandering off, but this time . . . *I'm going to give him a piece of my mind when we find him.*

"Patrick?"

Patrick jumped when his sister called out his name, maybe because the sound of her voice wasn't coming from behind him, but off to the side. He was starting to feel the chill in the air.

"Don't panic," he told himself as much as his sister. "The trail just split. You look over there to the right, and I'll check this way."

"All right," agreed Becky. "But just two minutes, and stay on the trail."

Patrick mumbled back at Becky and kept moving through the

bush. He pointed the way with his right toe, taking each step one toe at a time. He heard the sounds almost before he saw the faint glow of a campfire.

"Becky!" he called out. "I found something!"

Not sure that Becky had heard him, he hurried through the bush, pushing his way past branches and bumping into tree trunks.

"Give him back, I say!" came a small voice through the trees, and Patrick knew right away it was his brother. Was Becky behind him now? He pushed ahead.

"I told you" came Michael once more. "You're going to hurt him. Let go. You're cruel!"

Patrick burst into the light of a sputtering campfire, really just a few twigs. In the scuffle up ahead, Michael was jumping and complaining, reaching up to grab the small squirming bundle a man held high in the air. Christopher.

"Cruel?" The man laughed. "That's what they said on my old ship before the captain let me go."

Patrick recognized Officer York, but something was different about him. Something very strange. What had the *Victoria*'s sailor told them when the ship had come back to Goolwa with the ostriches?

Something about how bad he is when he's found a bottle.

By the way Officer York was acting and the crazy way he talked, there was no doubt the man had been drinking.

"But what do they know?" continued Officer York. Christopher struggled, but the man would not let go. "I'm the best officer they ever had, and what thanks do I get? I'm banished, sent away to this rotten little . . . puddle-jumping paddle steamer."

The way he spit out the words made it clear what he thought of his new job.

"Just give me back my koala, mister," Michael tried again. "Please."

"Give him back?" The man looked down at Michael, as if for the first time. "Sure, I'll give him back."

Patrick had seen this kind of thing before, back in school, when bullies would grab the hat of a small child and dance around with it, just out of reach. But Officer York was more than a bully in the school yard. He laughed once more as he held the helpless koala by the legs and twirled him around and over his head.

"Stah-ahp!" yelled Michael, and Patrick could hear the tears in his voice. But nothing he did made any difference. Officer York laughed and laughed. It didn't sound happy, though.

You can't do this! Patrick put his head down and charged into the clearing.

CHAPTER 12

Patrick's Surprise

"OOF!" Officer York crumpled and toppled backward when Patrick's head connected with his chest. Patrick held on and pushed hard, hoping to bring down the big man. Patrick didn't think past that. Just bring him down.

But it wasn't going to be that easy. The man fought back like a tiger. He held on to the koala by the back of its neck and took a swing at his attacker. But he missed and staggered backward.

"Stop!" screamed Michael. "Just stop!"

Patrick couldn't see much in the flickering campfire's light, but Officer York looked just as confused as he struggled toward them.

"Who are you?" he growled. "Put your fists up."

But Patrick wasn't going to play Officer York's game. Without a word he took a quick step backward, put his head back down, and launched into the man again.

"Ayy!" This time Officer York groaned and let go of Christopher. He held on to Patrick instead, grabbing him around the chest, then the throat.

The ground behind them must have given way, because the next moment both tumbled down a steep slope and suddenly hit the water. Patrick gasped in shock. He hadn't realized the billabong was that close. Officer York just bellowed like a water buffalo and nearly squeezed the life out of Patrick.

Patrick choked, gasped for air, dug his fingernails into the man's arm. . . . Anything to wiggle free. But it was no use. They thrashed about in the chest-deep water, slowly sinking in the soft mud.

He's going to choke me! thought Patrick. He yelled and screamed each time he came up for air, but the man only fought harder. Michael, who by now had pulled his soggy koala to safety, hopped up and down on the shore helplessly, waving his arms.

"Let go of me!" cried Patrick, trying desperately to get a better grip. He tried kicking backward, but only got stuck in the mud.

"Oh, so it's the smart-mouthed lad, is it?" bawled Officer York. Finally the man knew whom he was fighting. "Came to have me teach you a lesson, I see."

Not exactly, thought Patrick. But he knew he didn't want to hear any more. He gasped for air, took a second gulp, and ducked himself under the water for as long as he dared.

The man thrashed and fumed above him, but in the end could not hold on underwater. When he loosened his grip for just a moment, Patrick was ready and pushed his way to the surface as best he could. The mud tugged at his boots, but Patrick wriggled free and bolted for shore.

"You little worm!" bellowed Officer York. He lunged toward Patrick but missed. "You need someone to teach you some respect, you do!"

Patrick didn't answer. Michael was waiting on the shore and helped him up out of the water. *Good thing, too*, thought Patrick, pretty sure he could not have crawled out by himself.

"Come back here!" yelled the man from out in the muddy water. Patrick didn't look back. "Nobody makes a fool of Theodore York and gets away with it!"

"Hurry," whispered Michael. "Let's get away from here!" Patrick didn't need any convincing.

"If I get my hands on you, boy!" screamed York. He was still thrashing in the water as if Patrick were right next to him. Patrick wondered why the man didn't come after them, when suddenly Becky came running up.

"Whatever is going on here?" she wondered, but Patrick just spun her around like a top and pulled her along through the bush.

"We'll explain later," puffed Patrick as they hurried back down the trail.

"I'm really sorry, Becky," said Michael. His voice sounded even smaller in the dark. "You won't tell Ma and Pa, will you? It'll spoil the birth—"

"Michael!" Becky clamped a hand over her brother's mouth to keep him from finishing his sentence. She gave him a stern glance; Patrick could tell, even in the dark. "Now, tell me what happened. Why was Officer York there?"

"I don't know." Michael's voice started to break. "He must have been sitting there by his fire with that stupid old bottle."

Patrick nodded.

"I know Pa told me not to go too far from the *Lady E,"* Michael continued, hardly stopping to breathe, "but I was just looking for some fresher leaves, and we saw this fire, but I didn't see that awful Officer York until he grabbed Christopher right off my shoulder, and then he wouldn't give him back, and—"

"I saw that part," said Patrick, putting his hand on Michael's shoulder. They were almost back to the riverbank, and still Officer York had not followed. That was just fine with Patrick.

"I think we should tell," said Becky. "That man is awful—"

"We already knew he was mean and awful," interrupted Patrick. "You saw how he's been treating Jeff. And remember what that sailor said, how he gets even worse when . . ."

Patrick really didn't want to talk about it anymore. He looked over his shoulder, just to make sure.

"All right." Becky sighed and helped Michael up to the deck of the *Lady Elisabeth*. He was still gripping Christopher tightly. "Let's just get back inside. And you keep your mouth shut, little boy."

Michael winked at Becky and disappeared into the boat. Patrick tried to clean his boots off a bit, but Becky pulled him by the arm.

"You can do that later," she told him. "I think Ma is going to be worried about what happened to us."

"But I'm still soaking wet."

"We'll get you dried off."

Patrick shrugged and left his muddy boots on the deck. It wasn't like his sister to put off a chore, but he thought this time she was probably right. His mother was going to be wondering why they had taken so long and why he was all wet. So he followed Becky into the bright, lantern-lit salon.

"HAPPY BIRTHDAY!" everyone shouted, and Patrick nearly jumped through the ceiling.

"What?" He looked up to see his parents, Miss Perlmutter, Michael, and Becky all smiling and staring at him. The salon was decorated with homemade newspaper streamers, candles, and a piece of paper tacked to the wall that read in big letters, *Congratulations Upon Your Fourteenth Birthday!* Michael had put on a pointed paper hat and was clapping his hands.

"You little clown," laughed Becky. She mussed Michael's hair and looked around at the others to explain. "I had to put my hand on his mouth to keep him from spoiling the surprise. He was going to tell the whole thing."

"Oh, is *that* what you were doing back there?" Now it made sense to Patrick. "I was wondering, but I didn't think anyone would plan something like this."

Suddenly Mrs. McWaid noticed that Patrick was standing in the middle of a muddy puddle.

"Patrick. . . ?" she began. She bent closer in the lamplight to see what had happened to him. "I thought you were just going out to find your brother, but it appears you've been swimming. What were you thinking?"

"I'm sorry, Ma." He held up his hands. "I didn't mean to get wet. I'll get my other clothes on."

"And a hat," insisted Michael cheerfully. It looked as if he had long forgotten what had just happened to them at the billabong.

I don't know how he does that. Patrick shook his head but could not easily shake the image of the bellowing Officer York. He shivered while he let Michael balance a paper hat on his wet head.

"Honestly, Patrick." His mother dabbed his forehead with a rough, dry towel. "If we weren't celebrating your birthday tonight,

I'd probably send you to bed without dinner. No one else manages to ruin their clothes as often as you do."

What about him? Patrick looked over at Michael, who was trying to tie a hat onto Christopher's head, too. The koala would not cooperate, and Miss Perlmutter was trying to talk Michael into leaving the poor animal alone. *As usual,* thought Patrick as he walked off, *Michael is getting away with it.*

"We asked Jefferson to join us tonight," his mother called after him, "but he had engine room duty and had to work late."

"You asked him?" Patrick wondered.

"Of course. Isn't that what you would have wanted?"

"Uhh . . ." Patrick wasn't sure how to answer. "Sure, of course."

"But he said for me to pass along his best wishes."

Patrick changed his clothes quietly in the captain's cabin, putting on his only other pair of pants and a dry shirt of his father's that was actually too small for Mr. McWaid.

"Patrick?" asked his mother. "Did you hear me?"

"I heard you, Ma."

Patrick stared out the small window at the moonlight reflecting off the deck of the *Victoria.* And for just a minute he almost thought he saw someone staring back.

"Jeff?" he whispered, knocking off his party hat and looking more closely. But there was no one out there, at least not anymore. He turned to hear a rap at the door.

"Come on, Patrick!" Michael urged him to hurry. "We're going to sing now."

Patrick tried not to look over at the other paddle steamer as they were getting ready to leave early the next morning. Some of the crew were up and huddled in groups of two and three on the upper deck. Maybe they were watching the bright parrots in the branches of surrounding gum trees. Mostly they ignored anyone on the deck of the *Lady Elisabeth.*

"Jeff must be busy right now," Patrick told himself. He poured in an extra cup of grain for the ostriches as the *Lady Elisabeth* backed slowly away from the shore.

"It does seem qviet over there this morning." Miss Perlmutter had even noticed. "That loud officer, perhaps he sleeps late this morning, ja?"

"Perhaps." Patrick didn't want to think about York just then, and he was quite glad he couldn't see him. Maybe the man *was* still sleeping.

Patrick stared at one of the ostriches through the feeding door. When it pecked lightly at his hand this time, Patrick didn't pull away from the bird. Instead, he took some more grain and held it out for the ostrich.

"There you go." Patrick grinned as the bird slowly took its breakfast. "Don't be afraid. Everything will be all right."

Patrick knew he was talking more to himself than the bird. His hand shook, and he wasn't quite sure why. He just knew he would be glad to leave Emu Flat.

"Steam's up, Becky!" called Mr. McWaid from the engine room, and the big paddle started churning faster and faster, steadier and stronger. That was Patrick's cue. He jumped up to help, and after their mooring lines dropped free into the water, he pulled them up one by one. Firestorm growled at the wet "snakes" on deck. Patrick coiled them loosely as the *Lady E* nosed into the current.

Michael poked him in the side. "I'm almost fourteen."

"What are you talking about? You are not. Not even close."

"I'm older than you think." Michael was being silly. But then he looked up at Patrick with a serious question in his sparkling green eyes.

"What?" asked Patrick.

"I was just wondering what it feels like to be fourteen."

Patrick thought for a moment, then shrugged his shoulders and watched as they gradually put river between them and Emu Flat.

"I don't know," Patrick finally admitted. "I thought maybe I was going to feel *something* this time. You know, like feeling warm when you step out in the sunshine, or wet when you dive into the river? But it's the same as when I was thirteen. I should have known."

He wished it weren't so. But what else could he say? Never mind the delicious dumplings his mother had made for him from a bushel of tart apples they had bought in Mannum. And never mind the silly paper hats Michael had made for the birthday party, or the singing, or the poster on the wall.

I don't feel a day older, he told himself. He felt his chin for a hint of beard, something, anything, that would tell him he wasn't a child anymore. Of course, his face was as smooth as it was yesterday, no matter how much he wished it to be different.

"Oh." Michael sounded disappointed. "I thought you were going to have some wise thing to say now that you're an old person with an invisible beard."

"Ha." Patrick chuckled but didn't smile. From his spot on the side deck, he leaned out and looked back one last time before they rounded the next bend in the river. Down in the engine room, Mr. McWaid opened up the valves to full speed, sending up an even bigger spray of churning water and puffing steam. A minute later Emu Flat and the *Victoria* disappeared behind them in a Murray River haze that hung over the water like fluffy cotton.

"See you soon, Jeff." Michael waved his hand slowly.

"Right." Patrick looked down. "See you soon."

The pop of an explosion broke through the wheezing of their own engine, and there was no mistaking the *ka-boom* that rattled their windows. Patrick looked around in alarm.

"What was that?" he asked. "Was that us?"

Becky poked her head out the side window of the wheelhouse and looked down at them with a puzzled look.

"I heard that, too," she said. "I think it came from our engine!"

Dad! Patrick swung around the ostrich crates and raced toward the engine room, praying his father was all right.

CHAPTER 13

Rush to Echuca

"It wasn't us," Mr. McWaid reassured them, but he could not explain the sound. "Are you sure it was an explosion you heard?"

Relieved, Patrick scratched his chin and shook his head. "Becky and I both heard it, but . . ."

"But we're not quite sure what it was," finished Becky. "At least, I'm not quite sure."

Their father tossed another piece of firewood into the boiler and slammed the metal door.

"Well, then, I'd suggest we not worry about it. Probably just the *Victoria* starting up for the morning."

Patrick couldn't help shaking the feeling that it wasn't just the *Victoria* starting up its boilers for the morning. But he didn't know what else to do, so he returned to his daily chores. Cleaning up the ostrich cage was next. Somehow it didn't seem so bad.

"This is it?" Patrick looked out at the elbow in the river, just a day upstream from the firewood stop at Emu Flat. "This is really it?"

"This is the place, just back from the river a bit." Miss Perlmutter smiled and pointed west toward the hills that rose in the distance. "Karl will be waiting for us. Neuperlmutterberg."

"Noyberg!" cried Michael, swinging down on a rope from the upper deck. "I see it! There's a man in a wagon waiting for us. And it looks like a place where paddle steamers can tie up."

"Actually, young man," Miss Perlmutter corrected him, "Neu*perlmutter*berg is just a vays inland. Karl and the other men thought it was the perfect place for growing grapes. That vas before the mine vas discovered."

Patrick looked out at the bleak hills and wondered how it would be the perfect place to grow *anything*. But he would take the German woman's word for it; she was right about most things, he had to admit.

Becky blew the whistle, and, yes, there was a man waiting for them. A man and a woman, actually. He was dressed in a starched white shirt and black trousers, and she wore a matching dark dress with a prim white bonnet.

"Look at that." Michael pointed. "They look as if they're going to a funeral. Do you think they have a coffin in the back of the wagon?"

"Michael! That's just the way they dress." Patrick batted his brother's head and looked to make sure Miss Perlmutter hadn't heard them. But she was at the front of the boat, waving like a schoolgirl.

The people in the wagon waved backed solemnly, and the man slowly climbed down from the seat of the old wagon as the *Lady Elisabeth* approached the shore. Actually, he *did* look like an undertaker. Patrick knew better, though.

And when the horse slapped its tail at another cloud of locusts, it reminded Patrick why they were bringing the grain to the settlement in the first place; what little grass was left looked half eaten. A few more feet and the *Lady Elisabeth* scooped into the mud, nose-first, paddle wheels still turning.

"Noyberg!" called out Mr. McWaid, jumping to the front of the boat to throw a mooring line ashore. He looked back at Miss Perlmutter. "I mean . . . uh . . . that is to say, New Perlmutterberg."

Miss Perlmutter's face lit up. "Very good, Captain. You've

learned some German after all. I'm proud of you."

Michael followed his father but looked at the couple in the wagon with a frown, as if trying to solve a puzzle.

"How did they know we were coming?" he wondered. But a moment later he answered his own question by looking up at the column of black smoke trailing behind the *Lady E*. "Oh. I suppose they've seen us from a ways."

"Probably for at least the last hour," answered Patrick.

He scurried back to help Miss Perlmutter gather her things and get ready to go ashore.

"I hope it was worth the trouble," said Patrick, thumping one of the barrels. Miss Perlmutter replaced a book and snapped her trunk shut with a satisfying *clunk*.

"More than you know, child. More than you know."

Patrick stood for a moment, wondering whether Miss Perlmutter was talking about the grain or what was hidden inside the barrels. Not that they'd really had any need for hiding the Confederate rifles, he thought. They could have kept them in plain paper sacks and no one would have worried about it—not even the ostrich thieves, probably. Who had even suspected? Still, he guessed the German woman had been right to hide them. It could have been much worse. Better to be safe.

"Lend a hand here, Patrick!" shouted Mr. McWaid. He and the man from the wagon were setting up the *Lady E*'s crane, getting ready to off-load the barrels from the paddle steamer's deck to the wagon. The woman in the dark dress and white bonnet didn't budge from her place.

Maybe she's glued there, Patrick thought with a grin.

"Gerta!" The man from the wagon wiped his forehead and nodded politely at Miss Perlmutter. He spoke with the same clipped German speech as their passenger, and he arched his eyebrows as if asking a question. "You have arrived vith the *full* shipment?"

Miss Perlmutter crossed her arms before answering.

"Ja, Karl. *Everything* is here. You needn't have vorried."

"And this is the one with all the American rifles!" announced Michael, thunking one of the barrels with his knuckles. The German man's eyes grew wide, as if Michael had slapped him across the face.

"I'm begging your pardon?" he said hollowly.

"They know, Karl." Miss Perlmutter dismissed him with a sweep of her hand. "But ve can trust them. The McVaids have been very helpful. They're fine Christian people."

"And we wish you the best in your . . . uh . . . farming efforts here," added Mr. McWaid.

"I thought they were digging a copper mine," added Michael.

Miss Perlmutter chuckled and patted Michael on the head.

Karl didn't look too sure, but he said nothing else as they unloaded the rest of the barrels. Michael looked disappointed when the man didn't want to see the ostriches, but Patrick thought it was just as well.

"Why do you keep looking back at the river, Patrick?" wondered Becky as they unloaded the last barrel.

"What? Oh, I don't know." But Becky seemed to guess.

"I was thinking they would be right behind us, too," she told him.

That wasn't quite it. At least, Patrick was pretty sure Becky was thinking of the *Victoria* differently than he was. When she looked downriver, she was waiting. Hoping, even.

But Patrick shivered when he imagined the way Officer York might still be shouting at Jefferson. Or worse, maybe.

"I don't know what he's trying to prove," Patrick whispered.

With a sigh Patrick picked up the end of the rope that tied them to a single old tree on the bank.

Ready to go? He looked up at the wheelhouse.

"Gott bless you, Master Patrick."

When Patrick turned, Miss Perlmutter was holding out her thick hand in good-bye, and she looked just as she had the first time he had seen her back on the wharf at Goolwa. Straight-backed and serious, only this time her eyes looked a little softer. And the edges of a smile decorated her square jaw. Patrick took her hand and smiled back.

"You're a fine young man." She wouldn't let go of his hand, but

Patrick didn't pull it away, either. "Just be patient. And take care of those awful birds, ja?"

"They're not so awful," countered Patrick, smiling.

"Just be patient." Patrick couldn't get Miss Perlmutter's words out of his mind.

Be patient about what? There was plenty of time to wonder during the days to follow as they wound their way upriver past Wentworth, then past Swan Hill, and finally through the flat plains country that stretched out for miles around Echuca with a fierce, stark beauty. Patrick didn't mind the chilly, off-and-on drizzle, especially now that the ostriches seemed to turn their heads to listen when he talked to them.

"Think the *Victoria* is back there?" Patrick asked the biggest of the remaining ostriches on a morning when pale gold sunshine had replaced the drizzle. The bright-eyed bird looked a lot like the one Patrick had ridden through the streets of Mannum, only smaller. It stared at Patrick for a moment through the window of its crate, cocked its head to the side, and gently pecked at one of the freckles on Patrick's wrist. Probably looking for another of the treats—pieces of fruit, even sugar—that Patrick had been spoiling them with recently.

Patrick let his mind wander, and he kept expecting to hear the *Victoria*'s long, low whistle and see the mighty paddle steamer overtake them, but . . .

"You've been so quiet lately." His mother held his chin and looked straight into his eyes later the same morning. "Are you ill, Patrick? Not telling us something?"

"No, Ma." Patrick shook his chin loose and looked away. Even if there had been something he could explain, he wasn't sure he could tell her. Just an anxious feeling, as if something terrible was about to happen. How could he tell his mother that? It sounded silly.

"Ever since we left Emu Flat"—she fiercely stirred the steaming pot of oatmeal on the stove—"you haven't said more than ten words. Other than talking to those birds all day long."

"I thought I was supposed to take care of them."

"Yes, of course. And you're doing a wonderful job."

"Really?"

Patrick's mother waited for a moment, then looked at him again and frowned. "You still miss your friend, is that it?"

Patrick looked away but had to nod his head. Yes, he did.

"You and Jefferson went through a lot together."

How could he answer that? Of course they had.

"Well, dear," she continued, "you'll probably see him when we arrive in Echuca tonight. Your father thinks the *Victoria* is coming in just behind us. They must have been slowed down by something. Becky's seen their smoke a few times when the weather has been clear, following us just a few miles downriver."

Patrick expected that he probably should have felt more excited about the chance to see Jefferson again. He should have been looking forward to going back to Echuca, too. After all, it had been the closest thing to home they'd had since leaving Ireland—besides the *Lady Elisabeth* herself.

But with every hour that passed, he found himself pacing the decks more and more.

"What is *wrong* with you?" asked Becky as Patrick wrapped the mooring line tightly in place and they finally snugged up against the huge Echuca wharf that evening. "You look as if you've just robbed a bank, for goodness' sake."

The river was fairly high, so the wharf didn't tower over them as it often did. Even so, the wharf was wide enough and big enough for all of the many paddle steamers that came calling at the busy river port. That's what made it such an interesting place. But not this time, not for Patrick.

"Maybe it's the weather," offered Patrick as he looked up at the patchy gray clouds. They had just dumped enough rain to turn Echuca's High Street to dark brown mud. As Becky studied him, Patrick felt as if he were in the doctor's office for an examination, and he didn't like it.

"I think I saw smoke from the *Victoria*," she said. "Did Pa tell you?"

"I heard." Patrick nodded and grabbed another heavy line to tie up the front end of the *Lady E*. He tossed it up to a man on the wharf.

"Excuse me, miss." The young man on the wharf leaned down. "Did I hear you mention the *Victoria*?

Becky nodded, and Patrick's face clouded over.

"We've been hearing stories the past day or two about something that happened downriver. Rider on a stage passed along the story. Says there's been a man killed."

"Who?" Becky and Patrick asked in chorus.

DARK RUMORS

But the man only shook his head at Patrick and Becky's question. "I was hoping you could tell *me*. All I've heard is that it may be an officer, and that the accident happened at a little wood stop called Emu Flat."

"An officer?" asked Becky.

"Yeh, that's what they said. But a big boat like the *Victoria*, you know she's got a long list of officers. Could be anybody. Or nobody, maybe. Did you say you knew somebody on the *Victoria*?"

Patrick turned away, holding his head.

"Can't be," he mumbled to himself and turned away while Becky asked the man more questions.

"No . . ." His head throbbed with the thought of what the man was saying. *An officer on Jefferson's paddle steamer?* It could only be Officer York. He had the terrible feeling that this was no rumor.

"Woo-woo!" Michael came screaming across the deck and made a flying leap for the ladder up to the wharf. He wouldn't have far to climb since their top deck was about level with the wharf. "Come on, Patrick. Pa gave me enough money for a handful of lollies at Mullarky's store. He said to share."

"You go ahead." Patrick gave the mooring line a hard tug for good measure, then retied the knot so he wouldn't have to look at Becky. "I have to check the ostriches."

"Are you sure?" questioned Michael, but he was already up the ladder and gone before Patrick could nod his head.

The man on the wharf had turned to help someone else, and Patrick tried to escape inside. But Becky would not be put off. She planted her hands on her hips and blocked Patrick's way. "I've never known you to pass up candy, Patrick Ian McWaid. You're sick."

"Yep," Patrick shrugged and glanced down the river. "I figure I have a month to live."

"Don't be silly. Ever since Emu Flat you've been acting sick."

"You just heard Ma say that."

"No, I didn't. Now, you're going to tell me what's going on."

Patrick bit his lip until he tasted blood. Finally he looked up at his sister.

"Patrick?" She looked at him as if he were dying.

"I haven't told this to anyone," he whispered, looking around the dock. His father hadn't shut down the steam engine yet. His mother was busy inside.

"You need to tell *someone*." She grinned softly, the way only Becky could, and it convinced him. Now it would all come out. It had to.

"I think I've done something horrible. B-back at Emu Flat. You weren't there—"

"Yes, I *was*," she interrupted him.

"Not when I . . . pushed him in the water. You heard what the man on the wharf said. One of the *Victoria*'s officers *died* at Emu Flat. I think it was Officer York."

"Oh, Patrick." She pressed her lips together and shook her head, as if she were trying to explain something simple to a little boy who could not understand. "First of all, it was just a rumor the man was telling us. Second of all, even if it *is* true, you don't know who was . . . hurt, and you don't know what happened."

"I just have this feeling."

"Oh, come now. This is silly."

"Not to me, it's not. Maybe I'm the one who killed him."

This time Becky almost laughed out loud. "Patrick, you are *so* theatrical. There is no way that pushing someone into a waist-deep billabong could have killed him."

"It was deeper than that, Becky. Up to my shoulders, and it had even deeper spots. The mud kind of sucked at my boots. And the man was crazy. He had been drinking. I saw the bottle."

"I see that, but—"

"And we just ran away from him. Maybe after we left, he slipped down deeper into the mud, and—"

"All right, all right. I've heard enough." Becky held up her hands to stop him. "You'll see how silly you're acting when the *Victoria* arrives. I'm sure Jefferson will be able to explain exactly what happened."

Patrick frowned.

"You'll see," she told him.

"You'll see," Becky had said.

That's exactly what I'm afraid of, Patrick told himself. *I'll see, and it won't be good.*

He also knew that if he fell asleep, he probably would have bad dreams. At midnight he started pinching himself to stay awake, but that didn't work for long. The rockaby motion of the *Lady Elisabeth* at the wharf soon put him to sleep. Until he heard the urgent rapping on the cabin door.

"Mr. McVaid, Mr. McVaid, are you in there?"

At first Patrick thought he was still dreaming. But then he heard the voice again. A knock.

"Mr. McVaid" came the voice. "I must speak vith you. Something terrible hast happened."

Patrick blinked open his eyes to see Miss Perlmutter, standing with a sweater draped over her arm, at the door of his parents' room. Was it morning already?

"Miss Perlmutter!" Michael popped up like a cork and ran over to give the German woman a hug. "You're back!"

"Yes, child, so I am." She patted Michael's head and pointed outside. "Now, you're a strong young man. Vhy don't you give that sailor out there a hand with my trunk. I believe he needs some help."

"Yes, ma'am." Michael beamed and hurried outside, while Patrick squinted his eyes almost shut and lay still.

"Miss Perlmutter?" Patrick's father appeared at the door, rubbing the sleep from his eyes. "We're certainly glad to see you, but how did you get here? And what is it, six o'clock?"

Miss Perlmutter rubbed her hands together, looking more nervous than Patrick ever remembered seeing her. She looked his way, and he squeezed his eyes shut.

"Are you all right, Miss Perlmutter?" asked Mr. McWaid.

"Ja," she said. "I am qvite all right. But the poor officer, he ist not."

"I'm afraid you're going to have to explain what you're talking about, Miss Perlmutter. I don't see—"

"I'm so sorry. Perhaps I should not have come. But vell, you see, Herr Captain, the big passenger ship, the . . ."

"The *Victoria*?"

"Ja, the *Victoria*, it stopped at Neuperlmutterberg just a few hours after you left. A man asked if I vas a nurse, and I said, ja, of course I could help, but vhat vas I to do?"

They waited as Miss Perlmutter took a deep breath to continue her story. Something had obviously upset her deeply. Her lip quivered just a bit.

"But I could not help, no. Because vhen I came to the big steamer ship, they tell me thank you very much, but now I vas too late. They vould not even permit me to see the body. Not because I truly vanted to do such a thing, nein. But it vas all so very odd."

Mr. McWaid shaded his forehead, obviously trying to think it through.

"I still don't quite follow what you're saying, Miss Perlmutter. They asked you to help an injured man on the *Victoria*. Who was this?"

"A dead man, Herr Captain," she corrected him. "And may Gott have mercy on his soul. His name, that I do not remember. But they say he vas first officer."

"Officer York." Patrick's father nodded his head.

"Ja, York. That is it. That is vhat they said. York."

So it was *Officer York*, thought Patrick, straining his ears to hear every word.

"The men of course gave him a burial at Neuperlmutterberg. But they could hardly finish. The captain of the *Victoria*, he vas most anxious to hurry."

"So why did you follow us here?" asked Mrs. McWaid.

Miss Perlmutter paused.

"Follow? Ja, vell, that ist the odd thing." She shook her head. "The man who first asked me to the steamer boat, I heard him say to another that the McVaids should know about this."

"The McWaids?" Patrick's father sounded suddenly awake. "Are you sure that's what he said?"

"Of course I am sure." She sounded almost indignant, upset that he would even ask such a question. "Vhy else do you think I vould come to take care of you? But vhen I ask him myself, he says nothing more, as if his lips are sewn shut. No one says a vord, like frightened children. Very odd."

"John," said Mrs. McWaid. "Do you know why someone would say such a thing?"

"This is vhat I had hoped you could explain to me," said Miss Perlmutter. "But I must tell you, it vas almost as if Gott himself vas telling me to come to you. I could not say no. Understand it I do not."

"Did you just arrive?" asked Patrick's mother.

"Ja, but not on the *Victoria*. The captain, he vould not allow it. So I followed on the next steamship, just a few hours behind. I arrived hours ago, but I could not vait any longer to tell you."

Patrick felt himself shivering at the silence that followed.

I knew it, he told himself. *Becky was wrong last night. She was just trying to make me feel better. Officer York* is *dead!*

"Well, Miss Perlmutter." Mr. McWaid put his hands up in surrender. "I'm afraid you may have come all this way for nothing. We certainly have no idea why someone would connect us to Officer York's death. I still think the men could have been talking about something else."

"No, I . . ." Miss Perlmutter's voice quivered.

"You've come a long way," interrupted Mrs. McWaid. "But you should get some rest now. You look tired."

Their German friend sighed, and her shoulders sagged. Yes, she was tired. Very tired.

"Is there anything else, Miss Perlmutter?" asked Mr. McWaid.

Miss Perlmutter held up her finger.

"I learned one other thing," she said. "But it ist something I yet cannot prove."

Mrs. McWaid looked out their door and frowned.

"John, all this talk about that poor Officer York. The children may overhear. Don't you think. . . ?"

"Yes, of course." Patrick's father cleared his throat. "Come sit down in our room, Miss Perlmutter."

The door shut gently behind her, but Patrick could still hear the words.

"So many things vere odd," explained Miss Perlmutter. "But I came to understand that the captain vas looking for someone to blame."

"For the death?" gasped Patrick's mother.

"Naturally I confronted him, but he vould not explain to me, this old German voman. He vould not even talk about how the poor man died! 'Not your business. Get off,' he says. 'A sad thing,' he tells me, and pushes me out the door. No passengers on a passenger ship—very odd! Yet one thing vas sure—he did not vant to be blamed."

Of course not, Patrick told himself. *Not when it's my fault!*

Patrick lay for a moment longer, listening to the sound of the muffled voices behind the closed door and thinking. Becky would probably be coming down in a minute from the wheelhouse, where she had been sleeping. If she hadn't heard Miss Perlmutter—and it looked as if she hadn't—she would soon wake up for breakfast anyway. And Michael was still helping the men outside as they put away Miss Perlmutter's things. She would have to stay in the same place on deck, next to the ostriches. No one had come for them yet.

Patrick thought about Miss Perlmutter. What would be her advice in this situation?

"Vhen I vas a child, I spoke as a child, I understood as a child, I thought as a child. But vhen I became a man, I put avay childish things."

Patrick held his breath and dug his fingernails into his palms. Part of him still wanted to run crying to his parents. Part of him wanted to close his eyes and make it go away. Pretend all the horrible things hadn't happened after all. But that part of him was somewhere far behind now, back where he couldn't go. Not anymore.

I'll have to do it, he decided, *before anyone else gets in trouble for what I did.*

He dressed quickly, ducking low. It took only a moment to scribble a quick note to his parents, and while Michael was out of sight on the far side of the paddle steamer, Patrick was up the wharf ladder and gone.

He didn't know what else he could have said, and he knew his parents would find him soon enough. But he had to do it this way. Surely they would find the note he had left on the table next to the brass sink his mother used for cooking.

Went to turn myself in, he had scribbled. *Becky can explain.*

CHAPTER 15

IN THE LAW'S HANDS

"You did *what*?" An hour later Constable Fitzgerald looked at Patrick the same way Becky had the night before, and he carefully hung his constable's helmet on a peg above his neat oak desk.

Fidgeting in a wobbly chair, Patrick counted the shiny buttons on the man's jacket. It would hurt to look him in the eyes.

"Do you know what you're saying, boy? Do you know what happens to people who—"

"I didn't mean to." Patrick took another deep breath and started his story once more. "Honestly I didn't. But I was angry, you see, and I hit him in the chest, like this . . ."

The constable's eyes grew wider with each word. His assistant, a young man named Phillip, hovered behind him.

"With my head." Patrick didn't know how else to explain what had happened that night at the billabong.

"With your head?" Constable Fitzgerald absently stirred a third teaspoon of sugar into his steaming cup of tea. "We're talking about a dead man now, are we not? This is a serious thing here. A prison sentence, certainly. And you're confessing to this crime?"

Patrick nodded quietly. Constable Fitzgerald took a sip of his tea.

"Now, let me understand this correctly. You say that you are responsible for the death of one Officer York, who is—"

"He *was* the first officer on the *Victoria*."

"*Was*, yes. Never heard of him, and I daresay I know just about every sailor on the paddle steamers."

"He was new to the ship," explained Patrick. "They brought him aboard in Goolwa."

"I see. And you say this Miss Pearl—"

"Perlmutter."

"Whatever. This German immigrant woman can explain everything?"

"Not everything. But she's the one who told my parents what happened."

Constable Fitzgerald wrinkled his brow. "Now, *that's* what I don't understand. Where are your parents in all this? What are you doing here alone, a lad of . . . what, thirteen?"

"I just turned fourteen, sir."

The constable nodded and pushed his chair back from the desk, then turned to his assistant.

"Phillip, let's find out what's going on down on the *Victoria*." He took another quick sip of his tea and turned back to Patrick. "And you, young man, come with me."

"You mean you're not going to hold me here in the jail?" Patrick knew it sounded silly as soon as it came out of his mouth, like something Michael might have said. It just slipped out.

"Is that what you wanted, boy?" Constable Fitzgerald shook his head. "No, not yet. I want to talk to your father first. It's early. We'll see what's gotten into you."

"That's not going to be hard to arrange," the young assistant constable pointed down the street as he pushed out the door. "Looks like the McWaids are headed up the street, coming this way."

"Even better." Constable Fitzgerald leaned against the small counter in the front of the room, waiting for Mr. McWaid. Patrick slipped lower in his chair. There was no escape now.

"Patrick, what in the world. . . ?" Mr. McWaid looked seriously at his son for an explanation as he stepped in. "We saw the note you left. And Becky says something about how you think you're responsible for—"

"I'm so sorry, Pa." Patrick couldn't look into his father's eyes. "It's turned out to be such a horrible mess."

Constable Fitzgerald stood watching the emotional scene, stroking his mustache. From the doorway, his assistant caught his eye.

"Don't look now, sir, but here comes the skipper of the *Victoria* himself. Must have just got into town."

"Perfect!" Constable Fitzgerald's eyes brightened for the first time that morning. "Couldn't be better if I'd called them all myself. Get him in here."

The assistant looked outside again. "I think he's stepping into a hotel, sir."

"Well, fetch him before he does, man!" The constable rubbed his hands together. "We'll have this case solved before the magistrate even hears of it!"

Patrick's father put his arm around his son. "Don't you think we should have talked this over first, Patrick?"

Patrick nodded. But what could he say?

"I thought and thought about it, Pa, but there was nothing else to do. I just had to turn myself in."

"You're a brave lad, but I still don't understand why you wouldn't have come to your mother and me."

Patrick didn't want to look at the hurt expression on his father's face. Already he could feel the tears waiting behind his eyes, ready to betray him.

Not in front of all these people, he told himself. He looked up to see the constable's assistant leading a little stooped man their way. He wore a faded blue captain's cap and looked at them with dark, ratlike eyes.

"Here's Captain Witherspoon, Constable." The assistant burst in through the door with an odd smile on his face. "I told him the lad's story, and he's says that's exactly what must have happened."

One look at Mr. McWaid, though, and the assistant turned instantly serious.

"So you can confirm the death of your first officer?" Constable Fitzgerald sounded like a lawyer trying a case. The captain nodded as he studied Patrick with a cold stare.

"He was no swimmer. It's as the boy says."

"And the captain here told me a couple of his men will testify they saw the McWaid boy running from the scene of the . . . er, crime."

"So the case is settled?" wondered the captain of the *Victoria*. "We're free to go?"

"Not so fast." The constable held up his hand. "I'll need you to remain in Echuca for a few days until we can decide what will happen to the lad."

Patrick's head was swimming by that time.

This has to be a bad dream, he told himself. *I'll wake up, and this will all be gone.*

"Well . . ." The captain crossed his arms. "I'd expect, then, that you'll keep him locked up here in the meantime, no? After all—"

"No," interrupted Constable Fitzgerald. "I don't think it would be right, at least not in this case."

Instead, he turned to Patrick and squared back his shoulders. Patrick's father closed his arm even more tightly around his son.

"Patrick McWaid," chanted the constable, "I am placing you under house arrest for the murder of First Officer . . ."

He looked to the captain for help.

"Ted York."

"Theodore York," continued the constable, "of the paddle steamer *Victoria*. You shall remain in the custody of your parents here in Echuca until such time as the local magistrate determines a trial date. He'll be back in town tomorrow morning. Be here at nine o'clock sharp. Understood?"

"B-but . . ." the captain sputtered. "House arrest?"

"A kind of house arrest." Constable Fitzgerald licked his lips and pointed at them for effect. "That's my decision."

Fitzgerald's assistant shrugged as the captain stomped down the street. Mr. McWaid nodded, and they left without another word.

Anything but this. Patrick stumbled down the street but did not see anything. He relied on his father to guide him under the store verandas, past the horses and carriages, the bustling traffic of the river port. They were almost back to the wharf when someone ran up behind them.

"Well, look who's back in town!" whooped a familiar voice. Patrick stopped and turned to see a boy about his own age but more wiry and muscled. The boy's knees poked through his pants as if he had been doing a lot of growing.

"Jack?" Patrick didn't mean to sound rude. He just hadn't expected to see him.

"Call me John Henry Duggan, if that makes you feel better." The boy smiled from ear to ear and slapped Patrick on the back. "Hey, I know we haven't seen each other for several months, but you look as if someone just died!"

Actually . . . thought Patrick. He looked at his father, who didn't answer, either.

"I'll let you catch up with your old friend." Mr. McWaid finally let go of Patrick's shoulder and started back down the street toward the wharf. "But I want you back on the *Lady Elisabeth* in ten minutes. We have a lot of talking to do."

The look Patrick's father gave him said everything. As in, *You know I trust you, of course, but you'd better be back on time.*

John Henry Duggan looked at the back of Mr. McWaid as he disappeared around a corner, then raised his eyebrows.

"Sorry, Patrick. Looks like this is a bad time, maybe? But I've been hearing all these stories from river folks about the *Lady Elisabeth* over the past few months, and all the grand things you've been doing."

"Not so grand, really," squeaked Patrick. Jack didn't seem to hear.

"Me and my father, we've just been cutting trees up the river in the Barmah Forest. Talk about ordinary. And hard! We're going back in a few weeks."

Patrick nodded as the other boy continued.

"But how about these muscles, eh?" Jack lifted his right arm and flexed a bulging bicep. "Sawing wood is good for the muscles, I'll say."

Patrick nodded again, and Jack finally stopped.

"You're not saying much, Patrick." He leaned closer. "Are you sure you're all right?"

Patrick finally took a deep breath and shook his head. "No, not really."

"Hmm. Your family all right?"

"They're fine, except for—"

"Oh, I heard about that, and I'm awful sorry." Jack finally softened his voice and rested a hand on his shoulder. "It must have been tough to lose your grandfather."

"What? Oh yes, thanks." Patrick decided then that he couldn't explain everything to Jack in just a few minutes.

"Well, at least you're not mixed up with the tomfoolery on the *Victoria*."

You have no idea.

"Heard the rumor?" asked Jack.

"I *am* the rumor."

Jack looked back at Patrick and scratched his head.

"You're a strange one, Patrick McWaid. Well, word is there was a big accident on the *Victoria*, but no one's saying anything. Sounds odd to me."

"So I hear."

Jack leaned closer then, as if telling some big secret. He lowered his voice to a whisper.

"Don't tell anybody I said so, but a fellow on the street told me he saw a body dragged off the *Victoria* in the middle of last night."

"Last night?" Now Patrick was interested. He thought he remembered Miss Perlmutter telling his parents Officer York had been buried.

Jack nodded his head. "And you want to know what's really strange? They don't take the body to the undertaker. They don't take it to the doctor. They take it to the Collingwood Asylum."

The Collingwood Asylum. Even the mention of it made Patrick shiver. The place where they took the poor insane people or those who had drunk themselves into craziness.

"Which tells me," continued Jack, "the body isn't a body at all, but someone who's still alive."

"Did he have a uniform on?" Patrick thought of Officer York's body dragged ashore in the dark of night. No, that sounded too crazy, especially after what Miss Perlmutter had said about the burial in New Perlmutterberg.

Jack shook his head. "Don't know. But I'll tell you something else that's odd."

CHAPTER 16

DANGEROUS MEETING

"Something else that's odd?" Patrick was afraid to find out.

Jack nodded. It was his story to tell, and he was stretching it out as far as he could.

"You'll never believe it," Jack continued. "But a sailor in a strange uniform comes knocking on our door, before it's even light this morning. Says they need my father to come fix something on the *Victoria* right away."

"That's odd?"

"No. I mean, everybody knows he's the best carpenter in these parts. It's just that they make him promise not to tell a soul. Big secret. He wasn't even going to tell me. But they promised him big money if he came right away. And they wouldn't even tell him exactly what kind of job it was, not until he got there. Naturally, I came along to help."

By that time the two boys had arrived at the wharf. Patrick could see his parents waiting for him. From the way his mother paced the deck, she was none too pleased, either.

"Look, Jack—I have to tell you something else. But there's no time."

"Meet you later, then? After breakfast?"

"Sure, I mean, no. I'm in trouble."

Jack looked over at the *Lady Elisabeth* and nodded.

"I can see that, even from this far away. Say, what's in those crates on deck?"

"I'll explain later. But look, I don't know when I can get free. . . ."

Jack raised his finger, as if he had a solution.

"All right, listen. My father and I, we're staying in town tonight. Actually, on the *Victoria*, as long as she's tied up here."

Patrick shook his head. "You're staying on the *Victoria*?"

"Honest. Pretty good diggings, eh?" Jack grinned his toothy grin and held up his hands. "They said we could have a room if we didn't mind the cargo mess, only I don't think they knew about me coming along. So now it gives me a chance to investigate a little more."

Patrick nodded glumly. He wasn't sure what Jack would be able to find out, but something was not right—that much he could see.

"But look here, you can't tell a soul about all this, all right?" Jack looked at him closely. "About the body and everything."

Patrick nodded, but that wasn't enough for the other boy.

"Promise?" Jack held on to his shoulders. "You have to promise me."

"I promise." Patrick mouthed the words and checked over his shoulder again. His parents were still waiting. "But I have to tell you—"

"You can tell me tonight. I'm running errands for my father today, but I think I can get away later. Maybe your sister could help? I'll ask her."

"No, Jack—"

"And if you want to find out what's really going on around here, you meet me at the Collingwood Asylum tonight at nine."

"But I can't." Patrick shuddered to think what would happen if the constable caught him sneaking off the *Lady Elisabeth* in the middle of the night.

Jack ignored the protest and just looked Patrick straight in the eye.

"See you there," he said with a grin. Before Patrick could say anything else, he had turned and scampered away.

"Oh, and Patrick?"

Patrick looked back.

"I *am* really sorry about your grandfather. He was a nice fellow."

"He was. Thanks."

Patrick had to think way back to remember the last time he had seen Jack and his family. It had been months ago, before Patrick's grandfather had died, far down at the mouth of the river. Long ago and far away, or so it seemed. But now, how had everything become so complicated? Jeff, the ostriches, "growing up," under arrest for murder. . . .

Under arrest for murder?! Patrick felt panicked and alone as he climbed back on board the *Lady Elisabeth*. His parents, of course, were still waiting for him.

"Was that your friend Jack Duggan?" asked his mother, her arms crossed.

Patrick nodded and looked to his father.

"We came upon him on the way back from the jail," explained Mr. McWaid. "Or rather, he came upon *us*."

"He's always been a wee bit of a wild one, hasn't he?" Mrs. McWaid hadn't smiled yet, but she looked at Patrick as if he were an injured animal. "I'm not sure that I'm pleased he found you."

"I don't know, Ma." Patrick bit his lip, trying to keep from crying. "I think he's . . . all right."

"Patrick, my boy. How. . . ?" His father's eyes brimmed with tears. Patrick hung his head, and finally he could hold it no longer. His tears dropped to the deck at his feet.

"I've made such a horrible mess of it," he sputtered, not wanting to explain the story about the billabong all over again. But his mother would need to know. "I surely wasn't trying to, but I suppose I just let my temper get away from me again."

"I was afraid of that." His mother shook her head sadly. "Becky told me the whole story."

"But I . . ." Patrick took a breath and went on. "I was just trying to take care of Michael."

"We know you were." Patrick's father folded him in a hug, and there was no scolding in his voice. No "I told you so" or "You should have . . ." Just a heavy sadness that made Patrick cry even more.

"We'll get through somehow," said Mr. McWaid. "We'll explain everything to the magistrate. God is going to bring us through this."

Maybe He will, thought Patrick, and his head throbbed. *But I sure don't know how.*

Patrick lost track of time as they stood there on the deck of the *Lady Elisabeth* listening to the rest of the town waking up. They talked about what they could do as a noisy steam crane started up on the far end of the wharf and men showed up to begin unloading another paddle steamer. Maybe the *Victoria*. Becky came out to remind them about the breakfast she had fixed.

"The porridge will be getting cold," she said quietly, but it really didn't matter. Now she was crying, too.

"But, John." Mrs. McWaid looked up to her husband with searching eyes. "Isn't there something we can do? It was an accident. He's just a boy!"

Normally the "he's just a boy" part would have made Patrick grit his teeth and protest. But not this time. He just held on to his father's arm, squeezing it the way he used to do when he was a little boy.

"We'll get through this, Sarah," his father repeated. "I know it looks bad, but we will."

"But what about the job they offered you back in Dublin?" sniffled Patrick. "Everything's ruined, and it's all my fault!"

Mr. McWaid started to say something, but just then Michael came across the wharf, sprinting as if his life depended on it.

"Pa!" he yelled. "You'll never guess what."

Patrick looked up to see Michael skid to a stop in front of them.

"Oh," said Michael in a small voice. "What's wrong?"

Mr. McWaid wiped his eyes with the sleeve of his shirt and tried to smile. "Don't you worry yourself about anything. You'll find out soon enough."

"Hmm, well," Michael looked from Patrick to his mother and Becky and then back to his father, "I went over to see Jeff down at the *Victoria*, see, and—"

"You did *what*?" His mother gasped, but Mr. McWaid patted her hand.

"It's all right," he told her. "I told him he could go ahead, as long as he didn't bother anyone and he came back by breakfast time."

Mrs. McWaid frowned but didn't reply.

"And I didn't bother anybody, Pa, honest," insisted Michael. "But Jeff's gone!"

"I'm sure the captain has plenty of work for him," replied Mr. McWaid. "Perhaps he's—"

"No, Pa, you don't understand. Really gone, for good. Not on the *Victoria* anymore. All they would tell me was that he jumped ship somewhere between Emu Flat and here."

"Are you sure that's what they said?" Becky quizzed, and Michael planted his hands on his hips.

"I'm just telling you what they told me," he insisted.

"Jeff would never do that." Patrick shook his head. "Something must have happened to him."

"It does seem quite odd," agreed Mrs. McWaid.

"Not just odd," said Becky. "Impossible."

Mr. McWaid stared out at the river.

"I think Becky's right," he decided. "The situation with the York fellow, and now this. Something is surely not right here."

"And—" Patrick nearly blurted out what Jack had told him, but then he remembered his promise not to tell. No, it wouldn't do to get Jack in trouble. Especially not until he found out more about the person at the asylum or if it was just a rumor.

Patrick's parents looked at him.

He sighed. "Never mind."

It would be a long wait until that night.

Patrick listened to the night sounds until he was sure everyone had pretty much settled down. For him it was a good time to pray, with quiet raindrops gently echoing the evening's earlier downpour.

Echuca looked pretty quiet, too, except for the usual paddle steamer sailors spending their earnings in town. Most of the passengers from the different steamships had left to take a train elsewhere, but a few were still enjoying a late dinner at Henry Hopwood's Bridge Hotel or at the competing Echuca Hotel. No, it was just a normal evening.

Nothing to be afraid of. The ostriches are asleep, too.

Even Miss Perlmutter had gone to bed early, taking up her place again on the deck, but under the shelter of the overhanging roof. She was none too pleased that the ostriches' owners hadn't showed up yet, but what could they do about it? And she'd insisted that she would stay with the McWaids until the "horrible misunderstanding" with the constable was cleared up.

Patrick held his boots in one hand and tiptoed across the deck to the ladder, trying to avoid any puddles. He hoped the ostriches wouldn't see him and rustle their feathers. He'd given them extra dinner that night.

Not far to the top of the wharf. The only problem was, he wasn't quite sure of the time. Eight-thirty? Nine? He would have to check in a shop window on the way to meeting Jack at the Collingwood Asylum.

He was just about to step up to the ladder when a tug on his shirt spun him around.

"Patrick!" whispered Michael. "Where are you going?"

"Michael," Patrick gasped. "Who taught you to sneak up on people like that?"

"You did. And I'm coming along."

"No, you're not. I'll be right back."

"But where are you going? Into town like Becky did?"

Patrick looked toward the side deck of the paddle steamer, thinking that they probably would be disturbing Miss Perlmutter. It wouldn't take much to attract his parents' attention, either. And what was that about Becky?

"I can't tell you, Michael. But I'll be right back."

"Are you going with Jack Duggan?"

Patrick sighed. "Listen, I'll do your dishes for you next week if you just keep quiet. All right?"

Michael thought it over but finally nodded. "You still have to tell me where you're going, though. What if you don't come back?"

"Of course I'm coming back."

"From?"

"From the Collingwood Asylum, but—"

Michael gasped. "But you *can't* go there, Patrick." He grabbed Patrick's shirt. "That's where they put the—"

"What do you know about the place?"

"Not too much. I've just heard stories about crazy people. People who start screaming horrible things."

"Settle down, Michael. You hear a lot of stories. And I told you I'd be right back. Why don't you check on the ostriches again?"

"They're checked. If you're not back in an hour, I'm coming to get you."

Patrick sighed with relief when Michael did as he was told and shrank back into the shadows. Christopher, it seemed, had disappeared on one of his nightly trips again. They weren't sure how he got away, but they would surely find him nestled up in the branches of a nearby eucalyptus tree.

Patrick hurried off across the wharf and didn't sit down to put his boots back on until he was all the way to the soft mud of High Street.

Now to make sure Constable Fitzgerald doesn't see me . . . at least until tomorrow morning.

He tried not to think of what the constable had told him about his "house arrest." Did that mean he couldn't leave the paddle steamer, or that he couldn't leave Echuca? He hoped he wouldn't have to find out.

But he *did* have to find out what was going on at the asylum. Because so far, nothing made any sense to him.

CHAPTER 17

CORNERED

Patrick ducked out of the way when a loud group of sailors passed him on their way back to the wharf. They were talking about borrowing money from someone until the next paycheck, about betting on something, about the new singer at the Bridge Hotel. Patrick pressed himself into the shadows and didn't breathe.

What am I scared of? Patrick asked himself. He wasn't quite sure. The sailors passed by, and he set out again. After two more blocks, he turned the corner in front of the asylum.

The plain, two-story frame building wasn't much to look at, but Patrick supposed the Collingwood Asylum wasn't built to impress. After all, most of the people staying there would hardly notice the architecture. They probably wouldn't care much about the peeling white paint, either, or the weeds out in front. Patrick could see only a couple of lights on inside. He settled down behind a bush and waited.

Forgot to check the time! he scolded himself and watched the moon between hazy, rainless clouds. It had to be nine o'clock, or even later. But no Jack Duggan. A man on a horse trotted by, and the horse pulled up short just inches from where Patrick crouched.

"What's the matter, boy?" asked the rider, patting the horse's neck. The horse started to wheel around, and Patrick could do nothing except hold himself as still as a statue.

A moment later the man spurred the horse on, and they disappeared into the night. Patrick finally breathed.

I either have to go in or go back, Patrick decided. *Jack or no Jack*.

That would of course be easier said than done. At first Patrick thought he would march right into the building through the front door, but he quickly dismissed the idea.

They'd throw me out faster than yesterday's trash.

Patrick kept to the shadows of the scrub Murray pines hugging the edge of the asylum property and circled around for a better look inside. Here and there he could see patients walking the halls, some talking softly, others a little louder. The sound of one groaning made him pull the collar of his shirt up to keep from shivering even more. And then a twig snapped behind him. His heart skipped.

"Jack?" he whispered into the darkness. The first thing Patrick saw was Jack's big Cheshire cat grin. The moonlight seemed to reflect off the other boy's large set of teeth.

"Thought you'd be inside already," whispered Jack.

"What do you mean? Were you just going to march right in there and start asking questions?"

Jack chuckled. "You'd make a terrible spy. Come on."

Patrick followed and nearly stepped on Jack's heels. Most of the windows were decorated with plain white curtains, some pulled to the side, others trimmed with bows. A couple more candle lamps came on. One ground floor window, though, lacked curtains and lamplight. Jack motioned to the window with a jerk of his head.

"That would be an empty one," said Jack. "A way inside."

Patrick swallowed hard. But what else had he expected? Jack quietly slid the dark window open and crouched under it, his hands forming a stirrup for Patrick to step into.

"Up you go," he whispered.

"Wait a minute." Patrick held back a step. "How do we know who we're looking for?"

Jack sighed. "Look for a fellow with bandages on his face. That's what my father said the other fellow saw. He's the one we're looking for."

A man with bandages on his face, Patrick repeated to himself. *A man with bandages on his face.*

And if they found him, what then? Start up a conversation? Inquire how he was feeling? Chat about the weather?

Patrick was afraid to ask. Jack motioned once again to his hands. Patrick stepped up, and a moment later he had crashed to the hard floor inside the dark room.

"Oh!" he whispered quietly. The floor smelled like a combination of strong soap and an outhouse, and he sat up as quickly as he could. Jack came tumbling over next.

"All right, now," whispered Jack. "Let's see where this mystery man is."

Before Patrick could stand, though, he heard a rustling in the corner of the room. At first he'd thought the bed there was empty, but now a dark shape threw aside the covers and flew to where he kneeled on the floor.

"Arthur!" cried a wizened old woman's voice. Patrick felt the viselike grip of frail, toothpick fingers on his arm.

"Uh . . ." he began, but a surprisingly strong hand clamped over his mouth.

"Shh," she demanded. "If they see you, they'll make you stay here, too. Oh, Arthur dear, I knew you'd come for me someday!"

What is going on? Patrick's head spun. *And where is Jack?*

"Mmm, mmm . . ." Patrick couldn't speak, couldn't tell what was going on, until Jack struck a match on the other side of the room. The sputtering light was both welcome and unwelcome; he clearly saw the wide-eyed surprise of the wrinkled old woman when she saw Patrick's face. And she let go of him as if she had just seen a leper.

"Why . . . why, *you're* not Arthur!" Her voice grew louder with each breathless word. "*You're* not Arthur at all!"

The woman backed up slowly as Patrick edged toward the door to the hallway.

"No, ma'am. I'm terribly sorry to have frightened you like that. We made a big mistake, and we're not going to hurt you, ma'am. I'm sorry."

The old woman let out a piercing scream just as Jack's match went out.

"Aaai-EEEEE!" She had good lungs. Patrick stumbled over Jack in the darkness.

"Come on!" Patrick tried to find the doorknob and pull Jack with him, but Jack held back.

"No, wait," he whispered. "There's someone coming."

"I don't care. I'm getting out of here." Patrick thought of diving out the window, but this time Jack held him back. The old woman didn't let up her screaming.

"Where's Arthur?" she demanded. "You're not Arthur!"

"Hush, Mrs. Howell!" a woman yelled from the hallway and pounded on the door. Patrick and Jack slipped behind the door when it cracked open and swung a short way into the dark room.

"But I saw—" began the breathless woman.

"No, no, Mrs. Howell. Mr. Howell died thirty years ago, remember? Back to bed with you now."

The door closed again, and Patrick tried to pretend he wasn't in the same room with old Mrs. Howell.

If I move again . . . he worried, but the old woman obediently shuffled back to her corner bed. A minute later she was snoring, and Jack tugged on his sleeve. This time they were out in the dim hallway without another sound.

The hallway seemed to stretch from front to back of the simple square building, with a plain oak stairway at the far end leading up to the second floor. Here and there, straight-backed wooden chairs had been placed for the asylum's patients, though Patrick wondered if they were patients, as in a hospital, or inmates, as in a jail. The plain white walls were bare except for a single stern portrait of Queen Victoria. Rather fly-specked and probably over twenty years old. At least it hung straight.

The nurse who had pounded on Mrs. Howell's door was nowhere to be seen. Only three or four of the inmates shuffled toward them from the far end of the hall, and they acted as if intruders walked into the asylum every day.

"Look at what I have here," demanded one of the men. He wore a frayed bathrobe and smelled as if he hadn't bathed in . . . Patrick didn't want to guess. The man held out his box in front of their faces; they had no choice but to look.

"They came in through the doors," he explained, and it was almost as if Michael or someone younger were speaking to them from the body of an older man. Patrick couldn't help feeling odd, but he politely examined the man's treasure.

"Nice locusts," remarked Jack.

One of the locusts sprang out just then, hitting Patrick squarely in the forehead and bouncing off the side wall.

"Stop there!" demanded the man. He dropped his box to the floor to chase the escaped locust, letting out the rest of them. Patrick and Jack backed away, only to run right into a young nurse with a sparkling white dress and pretty jet black hair tied back in a neat bun.

"What are you boys doing here?" she demanded, not crossly, but expecting an answer with her raised eyebrows.

"Oh no!" cried the locust man. "They're getting away!"

The woman ignored the insect crisis, and Jack and Patrick could not avoid her straight, level gaze. Patrick had no choice but to tell her the truth.

"We were . . . uh, looking for someone," he stammered. "It's very important that we find this fellow."

"Right," echoed Jack, shifting nervously. "Very important. Very, very important."

"A bit late in the evening for that." The nurse kept her arms crossed. "How did you get in here? And don't I know you?" she asked, squinting her eyes at Jack.

"The fellow we're looking for is from the *Victoria*," explained Patrick, sidestepping her questions. "We just had to see him, to make sure he was all right. It's really urgent."

"Really, really urgent," echoed Jack, his eyes glued to the floor.

The young woman's gaze softened as she studied the two boys, and Patrick tried to smile.

"He must be a friend of yours," she said gently. She started to say something else, then held up her finger. "This is bending the rules a bit. But I think the person you're looking for is upstairs. Wait right here, and I'll see what I can do."

Jack gave Patrick a wink and a grin as the young woman turned back down the hall, her heels clicking on the hardwood floor. Patrick wasn't so sure, but she *was* nice. Maybe . . .

She paused for a moment, though, before going around the corner to what must have been the nurses' office by the front door.

"His name was Pitt, wasn't it?" she asked innocently. "Or Pitney?"

Patrick's mouth went dry. They were talking about Jeff! Jack looked at Patrick, and he nodded.

"Yes, ma'am," answered Patrick, but he could hardly believe it. Why would the *Victoria*'s captain and crew say Jefferson had jumped ship when he was really here in the Collingwood Asylum? The nurse nodded and disappeared around the corner.

"Now I'm really confused," Jack whispered to him. "What's going on here?"

Patrick shook his head. "I don't know any more than you do, except Jefferson Pitney is somewhere in this asylum. He was working as crew on the *Victoria.*"

"Well, it shouldn't take too long for us to find him," answered Jack. "This isn't such a big place."

"You!" demanded the man with the box of locusts. Patrick looked back, and the man was on his knees, chasing his pets. "I need you to help me."

"Well . . ." Patrick couldn't think of a way to refuse, so he joined the man on the floor. They cornered one of the locusts behind a couple of chairs, but they were of course nearly impossible to catch. Every time he was almost upon one, it sprang away and flew down the hall with a *flip, flip, flip* sound. But it didn't seem to bother the man. He just chuckled and chased the next one, and pretty soon they were halfway down the hall, replacing locusts one by one into the man's box. Soon Patrick heard the clicking of heels coming down the hallway again.

He peeked up from behind a chair to see a prim, older-looking nurse quickly approaching Jack. Not the nice, young one. Her steely frown told Patrick she was not there for pleasant conversation. But he didn't think she had seen him yet. He crouched back down.

"You'll have to leave," the nurse announced to Jack in no uncertain terms. "Now."

Her gravelly voice reminded Patrick more of a prizefighter than a nurse.

"Oh, but . . ." Jack put on his most pleasant tone. "The other nurse told us we could see our friend. Jefferson Pitney? From the *Victoria*?"

"As I told the girl earlier today," insisted the nurse, "there is no Pitney or Jefferson here." From his spot behind the chairs, Patrick thought she looked and sounded just like a bulldog ready for a fight. And who was "the girl"? Could it have been Becky?

"But . . ." Jack tried once more. "No one from the *Victoria*? Really? I heard—"

"You heard nothing but false rumors. There is no one here from the *Victoria*. Never was. And no one by the name of Pitney. I'll see you to the door."

It looked as if Jack had lost the argument against the bulldog. She paused a moment, then whirled around. "Weren't there two of you?"

"Two?"

"Don't play games with me, young man. You had a friend with you, isn't that correct?"

Patrick burrowed down lower. Suddenly a door opened up behind him and he heard a gasp.

"Aaai-EEEEE!" came the earsplitting scream.

CHAPTER 18

Impossible Promise

Patrick knew instantly who was behind him screaming. His first reaction was to cover his face, as if he could hide himself.

"You've taken my Arthur somewhere!" insisted Mrs. Howell, and she grabbed him by the arm.

Patrick sprang up to get away, but there was nowhere to go. The Bulldog Nurse planted herself firmly at one end of the hall, her hands on her hips. Mrs. Howell was right behind him.

"I knew it!" declared the nurse. "Out, both of you! You've caused enough trouble."

But we're so close, thought Patrick, and he looked down the hallway of closed doors. What had the young nurse said? Upstairs? He shook off Mrs. Howell's grip. A few leaps through the startled patients in the hallway and he was taking the stairs, two and three at a time.

"You, boy!" growled the Bulldog Nurse. "Come down from there, or I'll call for the constable. Jane! Fetch Constable Fitzgerald. This is unheard of! Stop!"

But Patrick wasn't going to stop. Not now. Not when he was so close. He ran on but tripped over something and fell on his face in the dark hallway.

"Excuse me!" Patrick tried to get up, but someone was squeezing his leg, keeping him down. Worse yet, no one had any lights lit upstairs, and it was even darker in the narrow hallway than outside.

"Jeff!" Patrick tried to shout, but he was drowned out by Mrs. Howell's cries. Finally Patrick wriggled free, but not before the Bulldog Nurse's heels came clicking halfway up the stairs. With each step, she blew a piercing emergency whistle.

"Jeff, where are you?" Patrick called again, but he still couldn't make his voice heard over the other noise. And he couldn't see to open a single door.

"Shame on you!" cried the nurse, lifting him by the back of the neck as a mother dog would her puppies. Patrick wasn't sure how she could see him in the dark, but she hadn't wasted a second. "Shame on you, coming up here and upsetting the entire asylum! Now, you leave this place right away!"

"But my friend Jeff . . ." It sounded like a whimper. It was all Patrick could manage.

"How many times do I have to tell you and your accomplice? There is no Jeff here. I don't know who told you such nonsense. Now, GET OUT!"

This time there was no escaping the steel grip of the Bulldog Nurse. Never letting go of Patrick's collar, she marched him down the stairs, past the still-screaming Mrs. Howell and the locust-hunting man, and shoved him out the door. He landed in a heap next to Jack.

"Well, we sure woke them up," said Jack. "Didn't we?"

Patrick looked back at the glum asylum. Still no light escaped from the top floor.

"I know he's in there," mumbled Patrick.

Jack pointed. "Yeh, but so are they."

In the front office Patrick could plainly see the long, ghostly shadow of the Bulldog Nurse wagging a crooked finger at the young nurse who had told them about Jefferson. They couldn't make out the words, but it didn't sound at all pleasant.

"I think our friendly nurse is in a bit of trouble," said Jack, holding back in the shadows. "Maybe she should have left to fetch the constable like she was told."

"Looks as if she didn't need to." As Patrick pulled himself back into the shadows with Jack, he heard a cheery whistle coming down the deserted street. Even from a distance he could make out the tall figure with the helmet and the dark uniform.

"The constable!" whispered Jack.

Patrick wasn't sure he liked the idea of hiding from the police, but he still joined Jack around the back of the bushes as Constable Fitzgerald approached. The man stopped for a moment and held up his oil lantern, as if trying to decide whether he wanted to go in. A moment later he continued on.

He's either on his regular rounds, thought Patrick, *or someone else heard all the noise and went to get him*.

Either way, Patrick didn't want to stay there to find out. Obviously, neither did Jack. When the constable was out of sight, they raced each other, step for step, down High Street to the wharf.

"See you in the morning?" puffed Jack when they had nearly reached the river.

"No, wait." Patrick grabbed the other boy's arm before he got away. "Look, I don't want to do this again. Sneaking around, hiding from the constable. I don't like it. And have you been talking to my sister about this?"

"Sure, but your friend is in that place, isn't he? If it were you, wouldn't you want someone out looking?"

"Well . . ."

"He's locked up in the asylum, and nobody will admit it! You don't think he went crazy, do you?"

"No, of course not, but—"

"And you can bet they're not going to tell Constable Fitzgerald, and they're not going to tell the magistrate. Don't you see?"

"Sure . . . I think." But he didn't see. Not really. It still didn't make any sense to him. Patrick glanced over at the dark shape of the *Lady Elisabeth* and wondered if Miss Perlmutter could hear their whispers. Not if she was asleep, but . . .

"So don't worry about it, then." Jack sounded sure of himself, as usual. "I'll figure out what to do tomorrow. Maybe your sister can help get us into the asylum."

"Don't get her involved, Jack."

"I said don't worry." Jack punched him on the shoulder and disappeared in the shadows. Patrick took off his boots and crept back to the safety of their paddle steamer. The ostriches didn't stir. He opened the cabin door slowly, trying not to let it squeak, then stood for a moment to hear the silence. Miss Perlmutter was asleep. So was Michael, and Patrick was glad his brother hadn't come looking for him. Nothing moved up in the wheelhouse, either, where Becky lay. But a faint glow escaped from under his parents' door.

"Patrick?" came his mother's soft voice. "Is that you?"

"I was just going to bed, Ma."

"Well, you get some sleep now. Remember Constable Fitzgerald said the magistrate will see us tomorrow morning."

"Yeah," Patrick replied, then whispered, "How could I forget?"

As Patrick quietly lowered himself onto his cot, he heard the sound of whistling outside, and it was coming closer. A faint glitter of golden lantern light filtered in through the raindrops on the side windows of the paddle steamer. Patrick could feel the light on his face, but he kept his eyes firmly closed. He knew Constable Fitzgerald was checking up on him, looking down from where he stood on the wharf.

Early the next morning, Patrick dropped his boots and stared as Becky and Jack hurried back toward the rain-soaked wharf. Had they been to the asylum?

"Hey!" he said, feeling the heat rush to his cheeks. "I thought I asked you to leave Becky out of this."

Jack held up his hands. "It was her idea. I just met her on the way back. Anyway, I told you not to worry. Remember?"

Patrick sighed deeply and mopped the drizzle off his brow. "Well, did you manage to find out anything about Jeff?"

The look on his sister's face told him everything he needed to know. She lowered her eyes and shook her head. "I tried . . . twice now. But they told me the same thing—no patient named Jefferson Pitney, no one off the *Victoria*."

"Sounds like the same treatment we got last night," said Jack.

"I'm sorry." Becky tried to pat her brother on the back. "I tried every way I could. But this, this . . ."

"Bulldog." Jack filled her in.

"Exactly!" She gave him a nod and continued. "This bulldog of a nurse blocked the way into the asylum and wouldn't even let me in. Just 'no, no, no' and slammed the door in my face. Quite rude."

"That's when I ran into Becky," Jack explained. "I didn't think it'd be a good idea for me to show up at the asylum again, eh, Patrick?"

Patrick grinned at the thought. "Not unless you want to disappear in there, too."

Jack hit his fist into his palm. "Say, Patrick, maybe you've got something there. I could pretend I was crazy. . . ."

"You don't have to pretend," added Becky. He ignored the comment.

"They'd take me in, and I'd find Jefferson."

"I hope you're not serious," answered Patrick. With Jack, sometimes he couldn't quite be sure.

"Of course I'm not serious." Jack rolled his eyes. "But don't you see? This is all tied together. Becky told me about you and this Officer York thing, and your friend Jefferson disappearing. There's just too many questions."

"I know all about the questions," said Becky, "and I agree it's very odd about Jefferson. But I don't see how Patrick's . . . accident can be tied up in all this." She shook her head in confusion, and Patrick knew exactly what she meant.

"Hurry up, now, Patrick. Let's not dawdle." Mr. McWaid emerged from the *Lady Elisabeth* and motioned for Patrick to follow. "The constable said for us to be in the magistrate's office at nine o'clock sharp. We don't want to be late."

"Mercy!" Jack stopped short and slapped his hands together. Patrick thought he could be quite an actor when he wanted to be. "Nine o'clock. I was only supposed to be taking a short break. My father's going to wonder what happened to me. Look, I'll catch up with you tonight after work, all right?"

"By that time you can probably visit me in jail," mumbled Patrick, but Jack just waved him off.

"Don't you worry, Patrick. If that happens, we'll get you out of there—same as we'll get your friend out of the asylum. I promise."

"Shh." Patrick glanced ahead at his father, who wasn't paying any attention. "You can't promise that. No one can promise that."

"You don't have much faith, Patrick!" Jack called out with a grin. For a second Patrick wished he could return the smile, but he couldn't.

"Coming, Patrick?" asked his father gently.

Patrick gave his sister a little salute before he left with his father. That was about as much bravery as he could muster up. His knees felt as if they might buckle underneath him at any moment.

"Sit down, please." The magistrate motioned to two burgundy leather chairs set at angles in front of his massive oak desk. Patrick slipped into one of them. He couldn't remember feeling smaller in his life.

"You understand, young man, what a profoundly serious matter this is?"

CHAPTER 19

SIGNED CONFESSION

Patrick nodded at the magistrate's question about the "profoundly serious matter." Of course he knew it was serious. But for several minutes all they could hear was the loud ticking of an ornate wall clock and the shuffling of the magistrate's papers as he made his way through stacks of folders set in front of him. Constable Fitzgerald finally stepped forward and pointed out a neatly handwritten report on top of one of the stacks.

"I believe that is my report, sir," said the constable, nodding and backing away like a subject before a king.

The magistrate paused for a moment, adjusted his half glasses, and picked up the paper.

"Yes, of course." He cleared his throat and began reading quietly.

The man himself was hard to ignore. Probably twice as big around as Mr. McWaid, but not what Patrick would call plump, not for a moment. The magistrate was simply large, and he had a hard time fitting into his desk chair.

"You're very fortunate the magistrate happened to be in town this day," Constable Fitzgerald said to Mr. McWaid. The magistrate ignored them as he read.

I'm not sure if "fortunate" is the right word for what I feel just now, thought Patrick.

Thick, dusty, black leather-bound books with gold lettering on the spines lined several bookshelves on the wall behind the man. Normally Patrick would have been curious to read through the titles, but these all looked as if they had the same kinds of names: *Rules of Jurisprudence, 1865*, or *London Review of Legal Issues*. He turned his attention back to his hands and wiped his sweaty palms on his pants.

"As a matter of fact," continued the constable, "he leaves for Shepparton tomorrow morning, then on to Bendigo. Isn't that right, sir?"

The magistrate didn't answer. He checked the back of the report; it was blank, so he removed his glasses and studied Patrick without a word.

"I've read your statement to the constable. Two other men from the . . . uh . . ." He picked up his glasses and held them to his face without putting them on. ". . . the *Victoria*, they confirm that you were seen running from the scene of the 'accident.' Is that correct?"

Patrick didn't like the way he said "accident," either. As if it weren't really an accident. And he tried not to watch the man speak. With every word, his jowls—the loose flaps of skin under his jaws—flapped like those of a hound dog. Patrick imagined the magistrate baying at a fox in a tree or a rabbit in a hole. The worst part was, Patrick felt every bit the rabbit.

"Patrick?" When his father looked at him, Patrick realized he had missed something the magistrate had told him.

"Oh!" Patrick sat up a little straighter in his chair. "I mean, yes, sir."

He wasn't sure what he was saying yes to, but it seemed the only answer possible. The magistrate frowned and pushed the constable's report across the desk at him.

"Then what would you like to add?" he asked.

Patrick quickly scanned the paper. Everything was there: *Subject confessed to initiating an altercation with the deceased. . . .* He supposed that meant starting a fight. And it was obvious who the *deceased* was supposed to be. And then it went on to describe all the rest of the sorry details.

"Well, then?" The magistrate impatiently drummed his meaty fingers on the desk. "You said you would like to add something. What would it be?"

Patrick glanced over at his father, whose face was positively white. But his eyes were still warm when he looked at his son.

"Just that I'm very sorry for the way things turned out," Patrick finally blurted as he shoved the paper back at the magistrate. "I didn't mean to hurt anyone."

The magistrate sighed and took up a pen to scratch in at the bottom what Patrick said. He blew on the ink once, shook the paper, and handed it back across.

"Are you sure this is all correct, son?" asked Mr. McWaid a few minutes later, peering over his shoulder at the official-looking paper. The magistrate had written a number of fancy titles at the top, and in the corner was a spot for a seal.

Patrick nodded sadly. "I read it, Pa."

"And there's nothing else you'd like to add?" asked Constable Fitzgerald. "We want to make sure all the facts are recorded correctly."

Patrick shook his head.

"In that case I want you and your father to sign at the bottom. Right there." The magistrate tapped the paper, near the bottom corner.

But Patrick couldn't quite find the line where he was supposed to sign. The paper swam in front of his eyes, and the letters all blurred together. He found himself wishing for a leak in the roof so that rainwater would drip in and ruin the document. He even looked up at the ceiling. No such luck.

"Right here, Patrick." His father pointed to a line. "That is, if you're sure. Don't sign it unless you're absolutely sure."

Patrick aimed the pen and scribbled his name. The tip of his pen caught on the *W* of McWaid, and he ended up with a blob of ink on his last name. He left it as *Patrick McW*.

Just as well, he told himself. When he handed the confession over to his father, the blob ran all over the page.

"Sorry," mumbled Patrick, but his father didn't seem to notice. Mr. McWaid dipped the pen into the inkwell on the magistrate's desk, applied his name to the bottom, under Patrick's, and handed the paper back across the table.

"Very well, then," said the magistrate, scanning the paper with a frown. "If that's the best you can do. Now, owing to the serious nature of this crime—"

A rap on the window interrupted him, and he frowned as he looked to see who was there. Patrick didn't turn around, but the magistrate gestured for whoever it was to come inside.

"Captain!" The magistrate seemed pleased to see the visitor, though he didn't stand up. "Come right in. I was expecting you earlier."

Captain Witherspoon of the *Victoria* stepped inside the now crowded magistrate's office. He took off his captain's cap and stood by the door, rainwater dripping from a long gray overcoat.

"Just wanted to see justice done," said the captain.

Patrick could see his father's neck muscles tighten.

"Raining again, eh?" The magistrate glanced out the window. "Well, now, where was I?"

"You were discussing the serious nature of the crime, sir," the constable put in.

"Oh yes. I was going to say that normally I do not deal with juveniles such as this young man. And seldom do we see such serious crimes in this part of the country. That's why I'm going to recommend that the case be immediately transferred to Melbourne, where the boy may face formal charges."

There was a hush in the room, and Patrick closed his eyes.

That's it, then. I'm going to Melbourne.

The magistrate's decision didn't completely surprise Patrick, but it still hit him like a load of bricks. He held his chest, thinking he might stop breathing, while his father rested his hand on Patrick's knee.

"Fitzgerald?" The magistrate wasn't through yet.

"Yes, sir?"

"You or your assistant will accompany the boy on the next train. Understood?"

"Understood, sir. I should say, though, that won't be until this coming Monday afternoon."

"Hmm." The magistrate counted on his fingers. "Today is Thursday . . . Well, no matter."

"Ahem." The captain spoke up from behind them. "He'll be held in the jail, will he not?"

This time Patrick's father couldn't keep quiet. He stood up, red in the face.

"I'd like to say something if I may."

The magistrate simply nodded.

"Patrick is a good boy, sir. A bit spirited, perhaps, but always respectful and certainly not worthy of this kind of punishment. I believe this is all a mistake. But if we must go to Melbourne to straighten out the matter, then that is what we'll do."

"Your point, then?" prodded the impatient magistrate.

"My humble request, sir, is that in the meantime he be allowed to stay with his family."

"That's highly irregular . . ." began the *Victoria*'s captain. The magistrate held up his big hand and raised his eyebrows.

"Alexander?" he looked at Constable Fitzgerald.

The constable shifted uncomfortably but nodded. "I have no objection, sir. He's certainly not a risk."

"Very well." Finally the magistrate stood, and he towered over them. "It's settled. The accused will be allowed to spend the remainder of his time here in Echuca in the custody of his parents and Constable Fitzgerald—who will stay on the paddle steamer, as well."

The *Victoria*'s captain sputtered for a moment but didn't protest. Constable Fitzgerald took a step back and raised his eyebrows, then nodded.

"I'll have the paper work for you in the morning, Alexander." The magistrate shooed them all out with both hands. "In the meantime, off with you. I've a luncheon appointment I don't want to miss."

Patrick thought it was way too early to be thinking of lunch, but he followed his father and the constable out the door. The captain had already slipped out and had disappeared down the wet street toward Collingwood Asylum.

"Looks as if you'll be our guest for the next few evenings," Mr. McWaid remarked to the constable, but Patrick could hear the strain in his voice.

"So it appears." Constable Fitzgerald held his hand out to feel the lingering drizzle. Small talk seemed very much out of place.

But the rain was all right, thought Patrick. *What else could it be doing on the worst day of my life?*

The worst day of his life stretched to two days, then three, and as he stared at the rain running down the deck of the *Lady Elisabeth*, Patrick tried to imagine what life in a prison would be like. He offered a handful of grain to one of the birds and remembered the time back in Dublin when he had visited his father in prison. It had been horrible. His daydreaming was interrupted when Becky grabbed him by the back of the neck.

"Come on, you," she told him. "It's Saturday, and you've been sitting here with the birds for hours."

Patrick looked up, bleary eyed. "What day did you say it was?"

"Saturday." She looked him straight in the eye. "It's almost three o'clock, remember?"

Patrick paused. "Am I supposed to know what that means?"

Becky planted her hands on her hips and looked around. Mrs. McWaid was busy cooking in the galley, and Patrick had a vague memory that Michael had left with their father to attend to some business in town. He didn't know what had happened to Miss Perlmutter. Even Constable Fitzgerald had left them alone. He hadn't seemed overly concerned about keeping guard, though he had spent the past two nights on the *Lady Elisabeth*, as the magistrate had ordered.

"Three o'clock." She lowered her voice. "Don't you remember?

That's the time Jack told us your nurse friend goes to work at the asylum."

Patrick tried to think about what had happened over the past two days. Mostly it was a fog.

"Oh, you're impossible." Becky finally let him go. "We're going to try one more time at the asylum, and you are coming with me."

"Am I allowed to do that?" Patrick wondered aloud.

"The magistrate said you could stay with your family. I'm your family, am I not? Unless you're planning to escape."

"You know what I mean, Becky. I just think this might be a waste of time."

"You're one to talk about wasting time. What have you been doing with yourself for the past two days?"

"I'm sorry—" he began, but Becky cut him off.

"Don't tell me you're sorry. Just change your attitude. Now, let's go. This is the only chance we have to figure anything out on our own."

CHAPTER 20
ALL MY FAULT

Patrick hung his head like a whipped puppy all the way through the muddy streets. Becky didn't understand. It wasn't that he didn't want to care. It was just too hard. So he followed his sister to Collingwood Asylum, avoiding puddles and mostly looking down. She kept talking, but he really didn't understand everything she was telling him until they were standing just outside the building.

"What are we doing here?" he asked her, as if waking from a dream.

Becky looked at him and shook her head. "We walked all this way and now you want to know? You're an odd one, Patrick McWaid. Watch out for the Bulldog Nurse."

Patrick finally snapped to attention at the mention of the Collingwood head nurse. Her, he wanted to stay away from.

"All right, it's three o'clock." Patrick tried to sound as if he had been paying attention. Actually, he was glad Jack had been helping them. It *did* feel good to know someone cared. Problem was, Patrick couldn't convince himself that it mattered. And when Becky got that look in her face, like a private detective, there was no telling what would happen next.

"Right." Becky looked down the street to see who was coming—a bakery wagon and a couple of younger boys trying to splash each other in the puddles. And a well-wrapped young woman with a sturdy black bonnet, circling around the boys and drawing her overcoat a little tighter. She crossed to their side of the street.

"Right on time," whispered Becky, "just as Jack said."

Patrick thought he recognized the young woman. Then he remembered the crazy episode inside the asylum and held back for a moment.

"You're not going to let go of this until you find out, are you?" said Patrick, looking longingly back down the street.

Becky's green eyes sparkled when she grinned. "I just couldn't stand to see you just sitting on the boat moping."

The young woman drew closer. Patrick tried one more time, a halfhearted attempt to back out.

"Maybe I'll just wait for you back at the boat."

"Stay right where you are, Patrick McWaid." Becky held him back behind her. "You're not going anywhere."

The girl would have hurried past them without a look, but at the last minute Becky placed herself squarely in the middle of the foot-worn path that led up to the front door of the asylum.

"Excuse me?" Becky looked for the girl's eyes. "You don't know me, but I believe you've met my brother Patrick?"

Patrick tried not to look, but he couldn't escape the young woman's shy gaze.

"Oh!" The woman almost gasped and her eyes grew wider. "I don't think I'm even supposed to be speaking with you. My supervisor would not be pleased."

"Please." Becky put her hand on the other woman's shoulder. "We just want to find out if you know anything about what happened to our friend Jefferson Pitney. We keep hearing—"

"Did Jack Duggan put you up to this?" asked the woman. Of course, Patrick realized, she must have recognized Jack after all. Everyone in town knew him. And Jack had been doing quite a bit of investigating since his and Patrick's first visit to the asylum.

Becky shook her head. "Not exactly. Actually, he's my brother's friend. But he—"

The nurse put up her hand to interrupt.

"I'm really sorry," she told them. She peeked around Becky to make sure no one from the asylum had noticed them. "But I can't help you. I wish I could. But I would lose . . . I mean . . . Oh, I've said too much. I'm really very sorry. Good day."

With that, she pushed past Becky, who didn't try to hold her back. The nervous young nurse ran up the steps and paused without turning around.

"And please don't come back," she told them.

A moment later the door slammed behind her.

"It'll be all right," Michael told Patrick after dinner that night. He was trying to hold Christopher, who finally squirmed out of his lap and crawled off across the salon floor. At least with the rain outside the animal would probably not try to escape again. "You just watch. It'll be all right."

"Well, it sure doesn't seem like it's going to be all right." Patrick picked at his dinner and shook his head. "You weren't there at the magistrate's."

"But people are praying for you, Patrick." Becky's voice was hoarse, barely above a whisper.

"Who is?" Patrick demanded, stomping on a locust. He pitched what was left of the crushed insect as hard as he could out the door with an angry grunt.

"People at church. I heard they even had a special meeting. Pa was talking to the pastor. He's talking to a lot of people."

"Don't you notice those kinds of things, Patrick?" Michael wanted to know. "You act as if you're in a fog. Well, we have friends here in Australia, and you don't even know it."

"What friends?" countered Patrick. "Who cares what happens to us?"

Becky sighed, as if it hurt to answer. "Jack cares what happens. He's trying to help, in his own way."

"In his own way." Patrick didn't smile. "That sure describes him. Watch, he's probably going to pick up and leave in the middle of all this, with no good-bye. Just like Jeff. 'Well, have to go, mate!

Going to chop some more wood with my fathah.' "

"Patrick!" This time his sister stood up. "How can you make fun of someone who's trying to help you?"

"I didn't mean it." Patrick bit his tongue and slid way down in his chair. "Jack's all right. It's just that . . ."

He didn't want to sit there and cry in front of Becky, so he crossed his arms and pressed his lips together as hard as he could.

"What?"

"It's just that everything's going wrong, that's what." Patrick got up and started pacing the room. Maybe it would help to move.

"Pa said he thinks we can get this cleared up."

"Think so? Well, why does everything have to be so hard?" His voice raised a notch. "First Jeff leaves us. Then all the fuss with the ostriches. And now the poor birds are sitting up on the wharf, for goodness' sake, waiting for someone to come claim them. And what can I do except feed them every day and give them water?"

"You're doing all you can."

"Sure, I heard that before, when the first one died. But it's not fair. They need to get out of those cages!"

"What else can you do?" asked Becky.

"I don't know. And what about Pa having a chance to get his old job back and even better, back in Dublin? Because of me it's all ruined! What else can go wrong? Can you tell me that? Can you?"

Becky and Michael didn't answer. Becky looked as if she might cry, too.

"And if all that isn't bad enough for you," he continued, "then what's going to happen when they put me in jail for the rest of my life?"

Patrick smashed another locust on the floor as hard as he could, and the koala cringed in the corner of the room.

"You don't have to scare him." Michael went over to scoop up his pet. "It's not *his* fault."

"I know that." Patrick stared at the floor. They listened to the light, steady rain drumming on the roof of the paddle steamer.

Finally Patrick sighed and went on. "I don't blame Christopher for anything. Or the ostriches, or Miss Perlmutter, or Jack, or you.

I only blame me. It's all my fault."

It's all my fault. Patrick could think of nothing else when they walked to church the next morning. The words took over his thinking as he plowed straight through the puddles, up the middle of High Street, just as Michael would have done. Only, Patrick wasn't playing.

All my fault, he thought again as he shook the pastor's hand and tried not to look into the young man's eyes. He was glad his father was doing most of the talking that morning. But Mr. McWaid was smiling at people as if nothing were wrong. And when Patrick felt a pat on the back, he wasn't quite sure how to act, either.

"It'll be all right, mate," said a voice in his ear. For a passing moment Patrick almost thought it could have been his brother trying to annoy him. But the old man who had stepped up from behind was not Michael. His teeth looked yellow and his dark hair stuck straight up, but his handshake was firm and his smile friendly. Patrick tried to smile back, wishing the man wouldn't talk to him. Not today . . . please.

Don't say anything, he reminded himself, *or it'll surely sound rude.*

But the man wouldn't go away, not that easily. He kept shaking Patrick's hand, looking deep into his eyes.

"See here, mate." He leaned forward, close enough to where Patrick could hear his hoarse voice over the hubbub of people greeting one another. "I hear you've had a bit of a rough go this past week. Want you to know people have been praying for you."

Who? Patrick wanted to ask. *Who would pray for me?*

But he was afraid to speak. He could only nod, and his mouth went dry. Of course Patrick didn't even know the man's name, though he looked vaguely familiar. He finally let go of Patrick's hand after pushing a coin into Patrick's palm.

"Don't thank me." The man grinned. "My father, he was from

the old country, he used to always say *'Gott sei Dank.'* Heard the expression?"

Patrick shook his head.

" 'Course, I don't say it the same way my old German *vater* used to say it, but you get my meaning. 'Gott sei Dank' means 'Thank the Lord.' Don't forget now." The almost-German man gave Patrick a wink and disappeared into the small crowd of people.

"I'll remember," Patrick managed to reply as Michael tugged him toward their seat. When at last they had all sat down, Patrick turned around to see. The old man was nowhere to be found.

"Who was that you were talking to?" whispered Becky.

"I have no idea." Patrick shook his head. "But I have the odd feeling that something like this has happened to me before. People giving me money . . ."

His voice faded, and he remembered how a man had once given him money to get to Echuca when they had first come to Australia. He hadn't expected that, either. But that had been a different man, a long time ago.

Five minutes later he got up the courage to open his hand and look down at the coin. A silver florin, worth plenty, and the strange man had just given it to him. Just like that! He quickly closed his fist again before anyone else could see the unexpected treasure.

" 'Amazing grace, how sweet the sound,' " sang the others, but Patrick only heard the part about "a wretch like me." And while he opened his mouth and moved his lips, the words stuck in his throat.

Who was that man? he wondered while the singing gave way to the pastor's sermon. Once or twice more Patrick glanced over his shoulder to see if the man was in the building. Finally Patrick decided that he must have left.

"You should listen to the sermon," Michael finally whispered. "It might be the last one you'll hear as a free man."

"Thanks for reminding me." Patrick frowned and tried to focus on the sermon. But he could not stop thinking about his brother's comment, nor the mysterious coin that seemed to burn a hole in his sweaty palm.

Unexpected Friend

As the pastor's voice rose up and down in a sermon singsong, Patrick wondered if prisoners were ever allowed to attend Sunday services. He tried not to think about Emu Flat and what had happened there. And he surely didn't want to think about Dublin, about the job waiting there for his father. His mind wandered until something finally caught his ear. Something about locusts.

"Their farm—their lifework—was gone in less than a week," cried the pastor. "Destroyed by locusts, just like that."

He must have been talking about someone in the Riverina District, north of the river and a bit east of Echuca, where the locusts had hit hard. Maybe it was a sermon about judgment, thought Patrick, *for wretches like me*.

He looked up when the pastor snapped his finger.

"Just like that," the man repeated. "And so today we share this proclamation of humiliation and prayer for the locust plague and for those who have nothing left. No food, no farms, no future. Or so it seems. But there *is* a future. And think how *blessed* we are as I read the proclamation from the governor. . . ."

Blessed? This caught Patrick by surprise. *You mean somebody else is blessed. Maybe everybody else in this room, but not me. I'm going to prison tomorrow. I'm responsible for a horrible thing. I'm not blessed.*

It had never occurred to him that anyone else could have more troubles than he did. At least, not lately. And he looked down at his hand as the pastor went on, reading the proclamation, talking about the troubles some of the Riverina farmers were having, asking people to help with a special offering.

Blessed?

Michael looked down at Patrick's hand, but Patrick snapped it shut. On the other side, Becky didn't notice and neither did his parents.

"What do you have in your hand, Patrick?" Michael whispered in his ear. Patrick just shook his head until Michael reached over to pry open his fingers. Patrick shook him away, and their mother gave them a sharp warning look.

Still the pastor went on about the needs of the Riverina people, and Patrick tried to listen. And the more he listened, the more it made sense. For the first time in a long time, Patrick found himself thinking about someone else—about something other than his own troubles. And surprisingly, it felt good. Really, really good.

Thanks, Lord. He closed his eyes and smiled on the inside. *Sometimes I forget.*

So he remembered the good things, the sweet things. What it was like to live with his family on the Murray. The sound of distant swans, and the way the river rocked him to sleep each night. The smell of his mother's fried eggs in the morning.

Blessed? Me?

He knew he was. That's why when the offering basket came by, Patrick didn't even have to think about dropping the coin in. He stared for a moment, surprised at the sight, at the sound of the florin clinking in the basket.

That was mine? he asked himself. For a moment it had been.

Michael looked from his brother's hand to the plate and back again.

"Where did you get *that*?" he blurted out.

Patrick just shook his head and passed the plate on to Becky.

"That man, Michael. That stranger . . . Gott sei Dank."

Late that night everything seemed so much clearer out on the deck. Finally the clouds had started to roll away, and once in a while the moon showed its bright silver face. So did the stars, and Patrick pulled his jacket up around him to stay warm as he stared up at the heavenly game of hide-and-go-seek.

But Patrick was still trying to sort through what had happened that morning in church, the odd man and the coin.

He didn't hear the sound of running until it was right there on the wharf. Someone was in a great hurry.

"Captain!" came a muffled cry, and then knocking. It had to be on the *Victoria*. And sure enough, a lantern came to life inside the belly of the whale-like paddle steamer. Patrick watched and listened.

Ten minutes later the lantern had bobbed up to one of the *Victoria*'s upper decks and was snuffed out. Still, Patrick had the very real feeling that whoever had been holding the light was still there, in the place a lookout would have been. It was almost as if he could see the pair of eyes watching him in the dark, unblinking.

He can't see me, wondered Patrick. *Can he?*

Whether the watcher could or could not see, Patrick pulled back around the corner into the shadows. He shivered and thought about going back to bed, but that would only give him another chance to dream bad dreams. About Officer York chasing him through the billabong, or worse. He didn't want to think about it. And another noise up on the wharf caught his attention.

For a moment Patrick thought it was another messenger on his way to the *Victoria*. But this one was even more noisy.

Sounds more like a parade coming down High Street, thought Patrick, and he strained his eyes to see who was coming. Jack nearly knocked him down as he flew over the edge of the wharf, caught the ladder in one hand like an acrobat, and spun to the deck.

"What in the world?" hissed Patrick. He grabbed the other boy by the shoulders to keep him down and quiet. But Jack would not be held down.

"We only have a few minutes!" insisted Jack, his chest heaving. "Come with me!"

"What?" Patrick tried to resist, but Jack dragged him up the ladder and onto the wharf. He looked back over his shoulder with a worried glance, but the *Lady Elisabeth* was still dark. So was the *Victoria*, for that matter. But what if Constable Fitzgerald heard all the noise?

"Will you tell me what's going on?" Patrick's arm felt jerked out of the socket as they ran through the streets.

"We finally found your friend Jefferson." Jack didn't slow down for a moment. "He was right there in the asylum all the time. Just the way I thought."

"*We* found him?" Patrick was having a hard time keeping up and talking at the same time. "Who's we?"

They ducked through a back alley, waited behind a large trash barrel for a lone man on a horse to trot by, then sprinted down a side street.

"Remember the nurse at Collingwood who was going to help us the first time we were there?"

"Of course." Patrick nodded.

"Well, I saw her again just a few hours ago."

"And?"

"And she told me that they were going to move our friend tonight, and if I wanted to see him, I'd better come now."

"You're joking!" Patrick couldn't believe it. "She told you that? Why? She wouldn't help Becky and me."

"I sure don't know. But she looked awfully nervous. Her name is Mary. She made me promise not to tell Nurse Bulldog. Said she'd be fired if anyone found out."

"Obviously." Patrick shivered at the memory of the square-jawed Bulldog Nurse. He didn't doubt for a moment that the young nurse, Mary, was right. But he wondered why Jefferson would be moved away. Why the big mystery? And why was Jefferson hidden in the asylum in the first place? Why. . . ? There were too many questions. And not enough answers.

But this time he knew they wouldn't make the same mistake of entering the asylum through Mrs. Howell's window. This time the young nurse was waiting for them at the front door.

"I don't know why I'm doing this," she whispered. "So don't ask. Just hurry up and say good-bye to your friend before she comes back."

Patrick didn't have to wonder who "she" was as they brushed past Mary into the asylum. But Jack must have been more curious.

"Where did she go?" he asked, his voice echoing in the empty hall as they hurried toward the stairway.

Nurse Mary shook her head. "Something about talking to a captain. This whole thing is so strange. Are you sure he's your friend?"

"We'll tell you when we see him," answered Patrick, leading the way upstairs. Jack stepped on his heels.

"That's just it," called Mary. "His face, you see . . ."

It was plenty dark, but this time Patrick held a candle as they made their way down the hallway. Here and there someone had laid out braided round rugs, as if trying to make the place more homey. It hadn't worked. Especially not with the sickbed smell that filled the asylum.

"In here." Mary finally pulled them aside and fumbled with a set of keys.

"You keep him locked in there?" Patrick's hand shook, and he tried not to drop his candle when a splash of hot wax hit his thumb.

"That's what first made me wonder," she explained. "Mrs. Chandler—that's my boss—she told me no one was ever to know about this fellow. She told me he was a bushranger of some sort and that the police would come for him soon."

Patrick held his candle with both hands. "And you believed her?"

"At first." The young nurse fumbled with the keys. She had a soft, sweet-sounding voice. "But the police never came. At least, they haven't yet. So even though Mrs. Chandler always seemed to have a good reason, when your sister told me what was happening, I put the pieces together."

"Wait a minute." Patrick shook his head. "I thought you said you couldn't help us. When did you change your mind?"

"After church," Mary explained. "Your sister came by again on her own. We talked for a few minutes."

"I *knew* Becky would find a way," said Jack.

Patrick understood just a little more when the door finally creaked open and they saw the bed. It was tucked into a closet, really, hemmed in on all sides. Brooms and mops competed for space with the rollaway bed. The room smelled like damp mops and soap flakes.

"Ohh." Patrick turned up his nose.

"I'm so sorry," said the girl. "But no matter what it looks like, we've taken good care of him. Is he your friend?"

At first Patrick wasn't sure. Here was *someone*, that was obvious. But Jefferson? It looked more like an Egyptian mummy wrapped in sheets than the Arkansas farm boy they used to know. The body's face was almost entirely covered. Only red, blistered lips showed through.

"Jeff?" Patrick whispered and poked gently at the sheet where he thought the body's shoulder might be. The body moved and groaned.

"His medication . . ." began Mary. She stood guard in the hallway, holding her candle high. "He's going to be quite groggy. Perhaps we shouldn't have disturbed him."

But Jack bent closer to the body, as if he was going to whisper something into his ear.

"PITNEY!" he announced loudly, right in the body's ear. "WAKE UP!"

Patrick jerked in surprise while Nurse Mary gasped. But the body only rolled and groaned. Whatever the medicine was, it must have been strong.

"It's him, all right." Jack looked up at them and nodded.

"How do you know?" Patrick wasn't so sure, and he pushed aside a couple of brooms to get a closer look. The hair on the body's head looked about the right color from what he could see in the candlelight. And his hands, well, they could have been Jefferson's, too. But that's all Patrick could see.

"They never told me his name," said Mary. "But I overheard

Mrs. Chandler say it once. And she would never let him speak. Said the bushranger's speech would be too foul to endure."

Jack pointed at a striped jersey and pair of blue pants hung carefully next to the bed.

"Do those look like a bushranger's outfit to you?" he asked.

"P-patrick. . . ?" At first the whisper sounded much like the mystery patient's raspy breath, but Patrick bent closer.

"Jeff?" he replied. "Jeff, what happened to you?"

The body replied by holding up a shaking hand. When Patrick gripped it, he knew without a doubt it belonged to Jefferson Pitney.

"Patrick!" whispered the body. Jefferson's body. "I was wondering if you'd ever come to visit me."

"We're here, Jeff." Patrick squeezed his friend's hand. "We're here."

"I can't see you, Patrick . . . can't see a thing." Jefferson put up his free hand and tried to sit up, but Patrick held him down. "Ever since the accident . . ."

"Here, now," objected the young nurse. "You mustn't let him speak too much."

"I need to know." Patrick held up his hand and turned back to Jefferson. "What accident, Jeff? The men on the *Victoria* said you'd jumped ship."

"They said that?" Jefferson snorted, and it was a welcome sign of life. "What a lie. A big, fat lie!"

Jeff shook his head slowly, as if trying to clear his head. "But what . . . ah . . . what did I expect?"

"Look, I don't know when she's coming back." Mary shuffled out in the hallway. Jefferson didn't seem to understand what she was talking about, and he continued his story in a slow, weak whisper. Jack leaned closer, as well.

Collingwood Breakout

"It was the morning you folks left the wood stop," explained Jefferson. "York was in the engine room, yelling at the crew the way he always did, and—"

"Wait a minute," interrupted Patrick. Surely Jeff was too groggy and confused to think straight. "York? But he . . . he drowned."

"Drowned? No," Jefferson replied, taking a deep breath. "I don't know which York you're talking about, but this one was alive and well and meaner than a bobcat up a tree. At least that morning he was."

"So what happened to him the night before we left?" wondered Patrick.

A pause, and Jefferson nodded, as if he was falling asleep.

"Jeff?" Patrick asked again.

"What? Oh, right. So he came back to the boat all wet and muddy. Madder than mad. And that morning, he was in there pushing people around, making them fire up the engine way too fast. I don't know all that happened, but there was this explosion, and York was right there in the middle of it."

"An explosion," echoed Patrick. "That must have been the noise Becky and I heard. Was it just after we left?"

"That's what I'm saying." Jefferson nodded once more. "York, he was hurt really bad, I could see. I thought he was dead, maybe.

But I tried to go in there and pull him out anyway. And the whole time, there was popping all over the place, guys screaming to get out, and this steam . . ."

He held up his hands as if protecting his face. "This steam, it comes out of a pipe and hits me right in the eyes."

"Oh, Jeff," said Patrick. "I didn't know." Patrick realized then why Miss Perlmutter would have overheard someone say the McWaids should know about this—Jefferson's injury.

"I didn't know, either. But suddenly everything went black. Hurt more'n anything. Still does. Even more than when you hit me on the back of the neck with that ball of rope." There was a hint of the old Jeff in that voice, and Patrick could see a tiny grin—the only part of Jeff's face not covered by bandages. Patrick blushed.

"I was going to tell you, I'm really sorry about that, Jeff."

"No matter." Jeff chuckled. Then, more seriously, "It was nothing compared to . . . York."

"Did Officer York beat you?" asked Patrick.

Jeff nodded, and this time Patrick was glad he couldn't see his friend's face.

"I must have been the first one to get in his way," explained Jeff. "But I figured a man could—"

"A man could take it, right?" Patrick interrupted. "That's what you said before."

"Well, I thought I could. I didn't believe all the old stories I'd heard sailors tell on other ships . . . about someone being 'as mean as Officer York.' "

"But why didn't you tell me everything before?" Patrick wanted to know. "My pa could have helped."

"That's just it. I knew you'd tell your pa, and I didn't want him getting hurt, too, if he tried to do something."

"Sure, but . . . wouldn't anyone else in the crew help you?"

"They were all scared of him, too," Jefferson explained. "And anyway, I figured it would get better. Even though everybody else in the crew thought something bad was going to happen, just the way you said. You remember? You told me that back on the wharf at Goolwa."

Patrick nodded. He remembered.

"And," continued Jefferson, "look what happened."

"What *did* happen after the accident?" Patrick wanted to know. Nurse Mary was still pacing out in the hall.

"Well, there's not much to tell. Nobody would say what really happened with Officer York. Big secret. Me, I couldn't see a thing, and then they covered my face and made me lie down for . . . what, I don't know. Lost track of time, like I've been sleeping for years and years. I think it's the awful stuff this old nurse keeps giving me. She has this really gravelly voice, you know? Sounds like a . . ."

"A bulldog," Patrick and Jack finished the sentence. And Patrick knew then what he had to do.

"We're going to get you out of here, Jeff," he whispered back. "Jack Duggan is with me, too. Don't you worry about a thing."

"Jack?" Jeff weakly put up his hand. "I remember you. But why are you all here now?"

"This is a rescue, mate." Jack took the hand. "Your captain was going to have Patrick here thrown in jail for the murder of Officer York, if you can believe that. And what's worse, he had Patrick convinced he'd done it, too!"

"Really?" The voice was weak, weaker than Patrick had ever heard it. "But wait. Patrick? He didn't . . ." He said a couple of other things they couldn't understand, and then his voice finally trailed off completely and he began to snore.

Patrick looked up at the nurse. She had just checked down the hallway again, and her face was tight and nervous.

"That's all the time I can give you," she told them.

Patrick nodded. "Can you get us a wheelchair?"

Jack caught on to the idea right away. "Righto! A wheelchair!"

But Nurse Mary held up her hands.

"We have only one, and it's downstairs. Besides, he mustn't be moved. He's in serious condition."

"Maybe so," Patrick agreed. "But it's going to get a lot more serious if we don't get him out of here."

"But . . . I only let you in to say good-bye to your friend, not to steal him away. If he's missing when Mrs. Chandler comes back, I'll most certainly lose my job."

"Not when the constable finds out what's been going on here," replied Jack. "You'll be a hero."

"But this boy needs care."

"And what kind of care are they going to give him where he's going?"

She swayed for a moment in the doorway, then sighed and let them by.

"You'd better hurry, then," she whispered.

"You're wonderful," Jack told her with a smile.

"I think I'm going to regret this," she replied.

Patrick hoped she wasn't right. He blew out his candle and dropped it on the floor.

"Jack!" he commanded, glancing under the bed. "We've got wheels. You take that end, I'll take this one."

"Wheels, eh?" Jack swung into place. "Always knew this was a modern kind of place."

Patrick grunted and started to push from behind the bed, hoping it would roll easily. At least they could get Jefferson to the top of the stairs, and then they could figure out what to do from there. Jack tugged from the front end, and they squeaked and screeched out the door. The nurse held up her hands.

"You'll wake Mrs. Howell!" Patrick remembered the screaming woman from their earlier visit, but he kept pushing. He had to risk it. But then, worst of all, they heard the front door slamming downstairs as they reached the top of the stairs.

"Nurse!" barked a gravelly voice, shattering the silence like a rock through a glass window.

"What do we do?" Jack froze. He knew who it was, too.

"She's back early!" Mary dropped her candle lantern with a clatter, and it bounced down the stairs. "Oh dear."

Patrick would have hidden in someone's room, but Nurse Bulldog was too quick for them. Before they could turn, she was already on her way up the stairs. They couldn't go back to the closet; the screeching wheels on Jefferson's bed would have given them away.

Of course, Jefferson himself was sleeping through everything.

"Quick!" hissed their nurse. "Under the bed."

The best Patrick could do was slide under the rolling bed and hug his knees to his chest. Jack crowded in beside him and wedged sideways, and Mary pulled Jefferson's sheet down as a sort of curtain.

"Nurse, what is going on here?" There was no mistaking the voice of the Bulldog Nurse. "And to whom are you talking?"

"I'm sorry, ma'am. I didn't mean to drop it."

"I'm not talking about the candle. But I'll surely take the cost of a new lantern out of your salary."

"Yes, of course, ma'am."

"And what is the meaning of removing this patient from his room? You know my instructions."

Patrick looked down and could just make out the Bulldog Nurse's polished leather shoe tapping impatiently on the floor.

"I . . . uh . . ." The younger nurse struggled for an answer. "Perhaps he would be recovering better if he had some fresh air?"

It wasn't much of an answer, Patrick could tell. Nurse Bulldog snorted with impatience.

"You let me worry about this man's recovery, young lady. The captain said he's a menace unless he's locked up. Now, let's turn this bed around immediately and return him to his room. It's not quite time to remove him."

"Yes, ma'am. I'll get the other end."

"No, I've got it."

Patrick felt a shoe kick him in his side and took that as a warning. But about what?

"Hold on!" Jack whispered in his ear.

As the bed lurched around them, Patrick reached up to grab a handhold on the straw mattress. With his other hand he gripped one of the bed's legs and lifted his body up as best he could.

"What's wrong with this bed?" complained the Bulldog Nurse. She jerked and shook the bed as they scraped down the hall.

"N-nothing," stammered Mary. "At least, it was perfectly fine the last time I used it."

"It feels as if we're pushing a lead weight. Here, the wheels are stuck—"

"No! Really, they're fine. Just fine."

Yes, it's fine, it really is! thought Patrick. But he wasn't sure how much longer he could stay hanging there like a bat in a cave. The mattress above his head creaked, and it sounded as if Jefferson was groaning.

"Unnh," began Jefferson.

"He's waking again," noted the Bulldog Nurse. "I'll get his sedative."

"Uhh," moaned Jefferson. "Patrick? Where did you go?"

"He must be dreaming," said Mary.

"Nooo, I'm not," insisted Jefferson. "What happened to—"

"I'll put him away and get his medicine," she interrupted.

"Humph!" the Bulldog Nurse grunted. "Aren't you the helpful one all of a sudden. Fine, see that you do. Here's another candle. I'm going to check down the hall."

"But wait." Jeff mumbled something else Patrick couldn't understand.

Finally they rolled to a stop, and Patrick slumped to the floor. He peeked out from under the sheet as soon as he heard heavy heels clicking down the hall.

"Go quickly!" whispered their nurse as Patrick and Jack rolled out onto the floor and stood up.

"Not without our friend," insisted Patrick.

"But it's too late now," she objected.

"Patrick!" Jefferson started to talk, but Patrick held his hand over Jeff's mouth.

"Quiet." Patrick leaned closer and whispered in Jefferson's face. "You're coming with us, remember? But you have to be quiet."

"Oh my." Mary bobbed on her toes and held up her new candle as she looked down the hall.

Would the Bulldog come right back? See them down the hall? Without warning, Patrick blew out the nurse's candle.

"You've been wonderful," he told her in the dark. "Now could you please help us lift him up?"

"I can walk, I tell ya," insisted Jefferson. "Where are we going?" In the darkness he must have swung his legs out and off the bed. The next thing Patrick knew, the big American had tumbled in a heap onto the floor.

"Get him," cried Patrick, louder than he should have. He, Jack, and Mary fumbled in the dark to pull Jefferson back up to his feet.

"I told you I can walk," insisted Jeff, and Patrick pulled Jeff's left arm around his shoulder.

"Sure you can," replied Patrick. "So let's walk you down the stairway."

They felt their way back, Jack on the right, Patrick on the left. Patrick felt with his toe for the edge of the stairs. Jefferson stumbled and pedaled his heavy noodle legs uselessly between them.

"Oh, he's a real walker, he is," muttered Jack.

"He'll be better outside." Patrick shifted the load a little higher. "Let's step down now."

He looked back into the darkness of the hallway just in time to see the bright light of the Bulldog Nurse's lantern.

"Thank you," Patrick whispered to Mary, and then he turned his attention to getting their load down the stairs—quickly. Jefferson was babbling into his ear the entire way down the stairs and along the dimly lit ground floor hallway.

"I knew you'd come visit me, Patrick. Tell the truth, I was starting to sour on this place, feeling like Rip Van Winkle, I was. But I sure wasn't ready to hang up my fiddle, not quite yet. Not ready to give up, I mean. Fact, you'll have to tell your sister I've even taken to praying lately."

"Shh, later," Patrick warned, but Jefferson didn't seem to notice.

"That's right, Patrick. I've been doing a lot of thinking about what you and Becky believe, you know? And if I'd known what was really happening around here—you being framed and all—I surely would have done something . . . if I wasn't so drugged up. See, I felt real bad about the way we'd been arguing, about the way I'd acted lately, and I just *had* to apologize to you. But then you came along yourself and . . ." Jeff started to fade again.

"Shh. We can talk later," Patrick said as they passed one of the doors. But it was too late. The door swung open and a woman stared out at them with wide, frightened eyes.

"Arthur?" she asked. "Arthur, are you there?"

Not again!

Patrick quickened his step, trying his best to get by without answering. Behind them, at the top of the stairs, he could hear the Bulldog Nurse complaining loudly. This time their friend Mary was speaking back.

"I'm sorry, ma'am, but accepting the captain's money to hide that poor American boy, and then lying about the entire affair, well, that's just plain wrong, and I will not be a party to it any longer!"

"Why," the Bulldog Nurse sputtered, "it was simply a donation. And the captain told us it was police business. Now, give me the key so I can check on this patient."

"You *know* that's not true, ma'am. If it were police business, the police themselves would be involved. Now, I insist . . ."

"Keep going," whispered Jack, his teeth gritting. "Here come the fireworks!"

CHAPTER 23

SO CLOSE . . .

"You figure anyone will care I don't have my breeches on?" wondered Jefferson as soon as they were out the front door.

For the first time Patrick turned to check what Jeff actually looked like. Up to that point it hadn't crossed his mind. Jefferson was wearing a long-sleeved wool undershirt and long wool skin-fitting pants—and nothing else. Warm, yes, but not exactly modest. Still, no one else seemed to notice them as they dragged Jefferson away from the asylum. Maybe they had seen it all before, in and out of the loud hotels and pubs. And of course, the only people out at that time of night would be deckhands and other crew from the paddle steamers and a few travelers passing through town.

"I don't think you have to worry about what you look like right now, mate," breathed Jack, but Jefferson had fallen asleep.

Good thing, too, thought Patrick. Then he heard the scream behind them.

At first Patrick thought it might be Mrs. Howell, looking for her Arthur. But then it came again, and it was the gravelly complaint of the Bulldog Nurse.

"What do you mean, not HERE?!"

They could hear her plainly behind them, probably through an open window.

"There's the first fireworks, just as you said." Patrick stopped to catch his breath in a dark corner. "And she's sure enough going to attract some attention."

"What do you figure they'll do to us if they find him before we get to the constable?"

"Jack, don't say that," said Patrick. "We'll make it."

"I'm only asking. But I think they're really after him."

"Well, of course they're after him. We just don't quite know why."

Patrick knew Jack was right, but there was no use getting Jefferson all worried. The American seemed in and out, awake and then asleep again. But one thing was for certain—he was heavy, and getting heavier, as limp as Becky's old rag doll. Still, they dragged him as best as they could through the muddy streets, as fast as they could without appearing too obvious.

"Look that way." Jack nodded toward the wharf as they got closer to the river. "I don't think those fellas are out for an evening stroll."

Patrick saw three husky men hurrying from the deck of the *Victoria*, coming their way.

"Over here," Patrick told Jack. "I don't know if they've seen us." He steered them to the side so sharply that they nearly fell to the street in front of a tumbledown storefront.

Or at least, he thought it was a storefront. At that time of night, all the town's stores were closed down. The only establishments open were the hotels and taverns.

"Eh?" A man standing behind a serving counter and polishing drinking glasses stared up in surprise as they burst in through the door. Four more men sitting around a table in a dark corner were lost in a cloud of sharp-smelling cigar smoke and a game of cards. The rest of the stale, shadowy room appeared empty, but Patrick had no desire to make sure. He had never been in such a place, and he instinctively knew why not. The card game stopped, and five unfriendly pairs of black eyes sized them up—two boys and a mummy in long johns.

Patrick shivered, knowing he was as welcome in that dark place as an ant at a picnic. But outside it was probably worse. . . .

"Uh . . ." Jack was the first one brave enough to say something. "Good evening, mates."

The five pairs of eyes continued to stare. Patrick thought it was only this quiet in church. But he could hear the squeak of a towel as the man in front continued cleaning his collection of glasses. What if the sailors followed them in there?

"We were just out for a . . ." Jack stumbled over the words and started again. "We were just out walking. I think we're in the wrong place."

Definitely the wrong place, agreed Patrick, and they backed up slowly. He prayed the sailors from the *Victoria* had run past by then, *because we're not staying in here another minute.*

Jack obviously had the same idea, and they struggled back out into the evening air. Where were the sailors?

Patrick was ready to kick or scream for help, or . . . He wasn't sure exactly what he would have done, but he wasn't about to drop his friend and run.

"There they go," whispered Jack, pointing down the street with his nose.

Patrick sighed a huge breath of relief and turned back toward the wharf. "Good. They probably went up to the asylum to fetch Jefferson."

"They'll turn right around when they find out he's gone," Jack reminded him.

"But we're less than a block away now."

True, but Jeff was getting heavier with every step.

"P-patrick?" Jeff put out his hands when they finally stepped into the storage yard surrounding the wharf. "Where are we? What are we doing here?"

Patrick strained under the weight and kept walking as best he could. Flickering lantern light from the *Victoria* cast long shadows behind them.

"Can't talk," grunted Patrick. "But we're getting you home. We'll explain everything when we get there."

"That'd be good," cooed Jefferson.

When all that was left between them and the *Lady E* on the open wharf were the ostrich cages, two people suddenly appeared out of the darkness, sprinting their way. But this time there was nowhere to hide. Patrick straightened for the fight. So close . . .

"Patrick!" called one of the approaching figures. "Where have you been? The noise from the other paddle steamer woke me up, and Miss Perlmutter noticed you were gone."

"Oh, Becky!" Patrick groaned, and he could see right away who the other person was.

"Gott sei Dank!" declared Miss Perlmutter, rushing up to him. "Thank the Lord! You're back."

Patrick nodded. "Gott sei Dank, Miss Perlmutter. You're the second person who's said that to me today."

"Oh?" Miss Perlmutter raised her eyebrows, but she wasn't through with him yet. "You tell me about that later, but for certain your parents are going to have something to say about this, young man. Perhaps also the policeman."

"I'm sure they will," grunted Patrick. His knees were about to buckle under. "But first we need a hand here."

Patrick stumbled just as Becky and Miss Perlmutter stepped in to help with the load. Everyone swayed for a moment, then leaned up against the closest ostrich cage for support. Becky was willing, just not quite tall enough to wedge her shoulder under Jeff's arm as Patrick had done. She stood back to take a better look.

"Ahh." Jack crouched on the wooden wharf. "This boy is *heavy*."

"Jefferson?" Becky sounded confused as the mummy put out his hand.

"It's sure good to see you again, Becky—" Jeff's breathy voice stopped the conversation dead, and Becky stepped back in fright. "Becky?"

Even in the dim light Patrick could see her jaw drop. Of course, Jeff didn't really *see* her.

"Sorry," said Jeff. "I guess I don't look the same in my 'mask.' "

No one seemed to notice Jefferson's long johns. Becky's mouth worked up and down, the words not quite coming out.

"Well, thanks to these two fellows," continued Jefferson, "I now know what it's like to be a sack of potatoes."

"A *big* sack of potatoes," added Jack, rubbing his shoulder and getting back to his feet. "I don't think I could have dragged you another foot."

"And you won't need to, either." A man stepped out of the shadows and blocked their way to the paddle steamer. "Pitney is coming with me, and I thank you very much for bringing him."

Jefferson stiffened at the sound of Captain Witherspoon's voice. When no one moved, the man stepped forward, holding out his hand.

"I send my men up to fetch the Yank, and look who comes back with him? But then, I should have guessed you'd find him."

"I'm no Yank," mumbled Jefferson.

Patrick stepped forward. "He's not going with you."

The captain sized up Patrick's challenge and brushed him off. "He belongs on the *Victoria*. We'll give him a bed to rest on until he's better."

The captain paused for a moment. "Oh, but he hasn't been telling you any of his crazy stories, has he?"

"It's no crazy story." Jeff backed away. "I saw Officer York that morning. So did a lot of the others, if you ask. Or maybe they're all too scared to tell."

"Ah, poor lad." The captain shook his head sadly, as if he were actually sorry. "The nurses said you'd been imagining things. It's the medicines, you see. Next I suppose you'll be telling us you live in Buckingham Palace, eh? So how is the queen, pray tell?"

"I saw what happened!" insisted Jeff. "Medicine or no medicine."

"But you don't remember much of the past few days, do you, son?" countered the captain.

"Well . . ."

"You see?" Witherspoon leaned around Patrick and tried to grab Jefferson's hand. "He'll just be needing some rest, poor boy."

"What about Patrick?" This time Jefferson tugged back hard. "You can't let him take the blame for what happened to Officer York."

"You're delirious again, boy. Not in your right mind."

"Never been better." Jeff stiffened and raised his voice. "And I'm not going back with you."

"What are they talking about, Patrick?" Becky wanted to know, but of course there was no time to explain.

"Listen to me now." The captain looked around nervously, like a cat backed into a corner. He pulled a dull gray pistol from the folds of his overcoat. "I didn't want to have to use this, but I will. I have the legal right."

Jefferson stopped and turned his head. "What's he doing, Patrick?"

Patrick couldn't answer.

"I vill not stand for this nonsense." Miss Perlmutter straightened her back in anger. "Do you think you can go around pointing that gun at us as if ve are some kind of criminals?"

"Listen, woman, I am the captain of this ship here, and I will . . ." He must have realized how silly his words sounded. Which ship here was he talking about? The man's hand shook, and Patrick could see beads of sweat run down his forehead. "This sailor is under my command, and I say he is coming back to the *Victoria*. Now."

"Nein." Miss Perlmutter planted her sensible black shoe on the wharf. "He is not."

"Put it down, mister." Jack spoke up for the first time. He stepped toward the captain with his hand out. "The constable's not going to take kindly to this when he finds out."

But the captain would have none of it; Jack's words only seemed to set him off. He swung wildly, missing Jack's head by inches. Patrick would have tackled the man, but Captain Witherspoon took aim and held Jack with an arm around his neck. For an instant it reminded Patrick of the aborigines' coming aboard to steal the ostriches. Only worse. This was not Miss Perlmutter with an old Confederate rifle, and the captain was not pointing his weapon in the air.

CHAPTER 24

LAST ESCAPE

"Captain!" Miss Perlmutter was going to try once more. "Put your veapon avay. Don't do such an evil thing."

Patrick took a slow step back, right up against the ostrich cage.

"The police constable," continued Miss Perlmutter, pointing over at the *Lady E*, "is right over there in the paddle steamer."

And a heavy sleeper, too, thought Patrick, wondering why the constable hadn't yet come out. Or his parents, for that matter.

"The constable," growled Captain Witherspoon. "What does he know?"

"He can settle this matter for us," answered Miss Perlmutter. "If you have the legal rights, as you say, he can help us find the truth."

For a moment the captain looked at his gun as if thinking it over. His hand was shaking so badly, Patrick guessed he was not used to aiming at people. Still . . .

"I've done nothing wrong," replied the captain, his voice quivering. "It was all his fault. Getting himself . . ."

No one moved. The captain looked serious. Crazy and wild-eyed, but serious.

"Whose fault?" asked Becky.

Patrick thought Captain Witherspoon might pull the trigger, his hand was shaking so.

"York, the young fool! But you think his father would believe it was his fault? No, sir. It'd all be on my head, I can assure you. Blame Witherspoon. And that'd be the end of me."

"His father?" asked Patrick. "Why would Officer York's father blame you?"

Captain Witherspoon harrumphed. It was not a chuckle or a laugh, for the man was not at all pleased.

"I'm talking about *Judge* York, the one who owns half the state of Victoria. He's going to need *someone* to blame for his son's death. Why not me, the former convict? He'd have my captain's license in a heartbeat, probably my head, too. Yeh, that's right. Blame it on the convict."

He looked at them, one at a time, pleading his case.

"Don't you see? I have a reputation to think about, you understand. A living to make. You think it's been easy, after working my way through a sentence of hard labor and beggin' my release? You, on the other hand . . . Ah, the judge'll have pity on you."

"You're horrible!" Becky raised her voice. "You would let my brother take the blame for something he didn't do just to keep yourself out of trouble?"

Maybe this man hadn't known about their grandfather, who had once been a prisoner. Or their father, who had been taken to Australia for a crime he hadn't committed. Or maybe he just didn't care.

"Who's saying he didn't do it?" asked the captain with a straight face. "And besides, it's your word against mine now. The constable already has a signed confession."

For the first time in a long time, Patrick didn't feel the least bit of anger. Just pity. Still, he couldn't just watch this happen.

"What I don't understand," said Becky, "is why no one else in the crew told the truth about all this."

"They're not stupid," Jeff spoke up. "They don't want the judge blaming them, either."

Patrick felt behind his back for the door latch. If only he could lift it up quietly . . .

"See, if the captain goes down with the ship, they go down with him." Jefferson crossed his arms. "The noble law of the sea, eh, Captain?"

"Sure enough we're a long way from the sea," replied the captain.

"So you were wondering how to explain what really happened," continued Becky, "when Patrick came along and solved all your problems. Isn't that right? He confessed to something he didn't do. An accident that you and Officer York himself were responsible for."

The captain pressed his lips together. "Sometimes Providence smiles."

"Now, this I cannot tolerate," put in Miss Perlmutter. "First you blame the child, and now you are blaming Gott for your own evil deeds."

Patrick thought maybe Miss Perlmutter was angry enough to hit the captain over the head with something. But before she had the chance, Patrick lifted the cage latch behind his back, stepped aside, and pulled open the door to the ostriches.

Run! Patrick would have yelled at the birds if he'd thought it would do any good.

As it turned out, he didn't need to. And Captain Witherspoon couldn't have reacted more surprised if Patrick had released a dozen lions. The man's face turned white as he stared at the giant birds that charged out into the group.

Miss Perlmutter moved faster than Patrick had ever seen. She dove to the side, away from the lead ostrich.

"Patrick, what. . . ?" Jefferson cried, but there was no time to explain. In the split second that Captain Witherspoon dipped his hand and stepped away from another ostrich, Jack grabbed for the man's arm. They rolled like a barrel on the wharf while Patrick hovered over them, looking for a way to stop the gun from going off.

"Off of me!" screamed the captain. "I tell you, I have the right! You will do as I say!"

At first Jack was on top, but then he was buried below the bellowing captain. In a moment it was plain Jack was taking the worst of the blows. Becky ran for the *Lady Elisabeth*. Miss Perlmutter tried to grab Patrick, but he shrugged free.

"Stand avay, Patrick," she ordered him, but he could not. It was too late for that. But what to do now? This was not Officer York teasing Michael about the koala. This was deadly serious. And the gun was pointed first in the air, then nearly straight at Jack.

"Patrick!" insisted Jefferson, leaning against the empty ostrich crate. The birds had disappeared down the wharf. "Tell me what's happening!"

"Just a minute. Just a minute." Patrick hovered like a wrestler over the fight, with Miss Perlmutter trying to drag him backward by his shirt. He didn't want to just jump on, though, because he would probably have only one chance. When he saw the captain's hand point away, he lunged forward and grabbed for the gun.

"Patrick, no!" yelled Miss Perlmutter as his shirt ripped out of her hands. He could hear shouting now from down on the *Lady E*. But he didn't see anything except Captain Witherspoon's red-faced rage, nose to nose. Patrick was sucked into the rolling, scratching fight, with Miss Perlmutter tugging and shouting at his feet.

"Mr. McVaid!" she shouted. "Mr. McVaid! Come qvickly!"

But where was the gun? The shouts seemed to blur around him. Jack pounded on the man's back while Patrick gripped the hand holding the weapon with both of his own hands, trying with all his strength to point it up and away. Captain Witherspoon was stronger than he looked, though—much stronger—and Patrick felt his own strength leaving him at just the wrong time. Even two against one, Patrick was losing the wrestling match. And Jack could do nothing from where he was pinned.

"Please don't do this, sir," whispered Patrick, staring into the captain's eyes. He couldn't remember ever pleading with anyone for his life. "You don't know what you're doing."

Captain Witherspoon trembled and paused for a moment, long enough for Patrick to get a better grip.

"Captain Witherspoon," pleaded Patrick. "Please, no. Jeff will tell everyone the truth about what happened back at Emu Flat. You won't have to take all the blame. Don't make it worse. Please."

But the gun dropped even lower, and Patrick could only close his eyes, wincing.

"Where are you, Patrick?" Jefferson must have stepped toward them just then; he stumbled over Patrick as the gun went off.

In the pandemonium that followed, Patrick rolled free and bumped into Jefferson and Jack. Miss Perlmutter was on them in a moment, gathering them up like a hen gathers her chicks.

"Boys," she asked them. "Are you all right?"

"I . . . I don't know," wheezed Jack. He was sitting up but still trying to catch his breath.

"Is someone going to tell me what. . . ?" began Jefferson, but he must have heard Captain Witherspoon's shocked voice.

The paddle steamer captain was on his knees, and all the fight had drained out of his face. He held the smoking pistol up and stared at his weapon as if for the first time.

"I could have killed someone," he mumbled over and over. "I could have killed someone."

"Captain!" cried Miss Perlmutter. Maybe she thought he would do more harm with the gun. But before anyone could move, he flung the weapon toward the river, high over the heads of the constable and Mr. McWaid, who were now rushing up from the *Lady E*. The pistol landed with a splash.

"Patrick!" cried Patrick's father. "Stay right there!"

Patrick would have, but he had already stood up and stepped over to Captain Witherspoon. And the older man didn't resist when Patrick reached down and gently helped him to his feet.

The welcome morning sun was out three days later when everyone followed Michael down the trail. Ahead lay an especially bushy grove of eucalyptus trees just outside of Echuca. Yesterday's rain seemed to steam right off the leaves, sending a glittering, minty fog into the air. It was a spot where Patrick could remember seeing several koala families.

"Do you really think Christopher will like it out here?" worried Michael. He held his pet on his shoulder for the last time. Christopher kept his nose to the breeze, and his eyes looked wider than usual.

"You said yourself there's plenty of other critters out here to keep him company, didn't you?" asked Jefferson. "Maybe even an ostrich or two?"

His face was still covered in bandages, so he held tightly to Becky's arm. Mr. and Mrs. McWaid were arm in arm, too, followed by Jack, Miss Perlmutter, and finally Patrick.

"No, Jeff," replied Michael. "We caught all the ostriches again, remember?"

"I'm certainly glad the owners finally came for the birds," added Mrs. McWaid, "after all that trouble. And I'll tell you something else. That was the first and last time I'll be talked into carrying big animals like that."

"They were fine, Pa," protested Patrick. But Michael had already caught sight of something else. He pointed straight up at one of the taller trees.

"Look over there, Jeff. Oh . . ." Michael put his hand on his mouth with a little gasp. "I'm sorry. I didn't mean to say 'look.' "

"Pay it no mind." Jeff put up his hand. "I'll be getting used to it. And even if I never see again, like the doctor says, seems like it's all right somehow. . . . And it sure helps to have a pretty lady leading me around."

Becky blushed, and Patrick wasn't sure it would be as easy as Jefferson was making it sound. He wanted to know more about what Jeff had started to say back in the asylum, the part about praying. For Jeff, it was a big step in the right direction. An answer to Patrick's own prayers. Finally it all made sense.

At least they would have time now to talk. Time on the river. And the thought of staying in Australia for good didn't fill Patrick with mixed-up feelings anymore. Dublin, Ireland, was far away and long ago.

"Well, we're happy to have you back with us to stay, Jeff," said Mr. McWaid. "Especially since we're not going back to Dublin."

"I'm sure sorry you had to pass up that job, sir. I feel as if I'm somehow responsible."

"Nonsense." Mr. McWaid looked over at Patrick. "We would have decided to stay anyway. This is our home now. So it's not your fault, not Patrick's, either, in spite of what he's said. Isn't that right, Patrick?"

Patrick took a deep breath to smell the sweet, damp perfume of the eucalyptus trees. Lately it had become his favorite smell, better than a candy store or even the salty ocean.

"Patrick?"

"Pardon me?" Patrick looked back at his father, who was smiling at him. "What was the question?"

"The question is, are you feeling better now that all the charges against you were dropped? Are you glad we're not moving back to Dublin? Glad to stay here on the Murray?"

Mrs. McWaid laughed. "That's three questions, dear."

Patrick looked at each face and thought about the lifetime of adventures they'd had on the river over the past months. The adventure of finding their father. Hiding from bushrangers. Taking the Prince of Edinburgh on a dangerous river tour. Helping their aborigine and Chinese friends. Saving the *Lady Elisabeth*. Escaping a firestorm, and an epidemic, too. And now this latest adventure with Miss Perlmutter, the ostriches, Jack, and Jefferson. So many memories . . .

Was he glad to stay on the Murray? A few weeks ago, he might have had a different answer. Yes, he was sure he would have. But things had changed. He had changed. He looked at Miss Perlmutter, and she smiled back at him with a wink of her eye.

"'But vhen I became a man . . .'" she began to quote her verse once more, and it seemed to fit very well. Very well, indeed.

Patrick finally nodded his head.

"I'm glad we're here, Pa," said Patrick. "It'll be nice to stay in the place where I really grew up. Nice to stay where I have friends. Gott sei Dank."

"Now, you tell me, Patrick McVaid." Miss Perlmutter waved a finger at him. "Vhere also did you hear that expression, besides from my own lips?"

So Patrick had to explain the story of the man in the church the Sunday before, the one who had pressed the coin into his hand.

"A Bavarian angel, perhaps?" Miss Perlmutter grinned, and Patrick wasn't quite sure if she was serious.

"I don't know. But if there is such a one, I found him."

"Or rather, he found *you*. And then he disappeared. Here, then gone." The German woman shook her head. "Maybe a little like this koala, eh?"

Michael was the only one who missed the conversation. A few feet away he had lifted Christopher up to the peeling papery trunk of the largest eucalyptus in the grove. Christopher, no longer a pet, looked back at him just once, as if to ask, "Do you really mean it?"

They did. And then Christopher caught hold with his sharp claws and scampered right up the side of the tree, up into the branches.

"Good-bye, Christopher," whispered Michael, misty-eyed. "Stay here with your friends. This is where you belong."

Patrick knew the feeling.

Beginnings and Endings

This adventure is about endings—and beginnings, too. The ending of ties to the old land, which many immigrants had to face as they began their new lives in Australia. The ending of being just a kid, and the beginning of something more. That's what Patrick learned.

It's also about the reality of pioneer life in 1869. And this story is built on several true stories. For instance, the story of the ostriches coming to Australia is based on fact. The first ostriches were actually imported to Australia in 1869, with the idea of raising more birds to help meet the worldwide demand for fashionable ostrich plumes. The first imported birds had a tough go of it, and the fashion faded out at the turn of the century. But today many Australian farmers still raise ostriches for the birds' meat. So do farmers all over the world.

Miss Perlmutter is like many of the German immigrants who came to Australia in the mid- to late 1800s. Other than the British Isles, Germany sent more immigrants during this period than any other country. Often German settlers founded their own communities in the fertile valleys around Adelaide, not far from the Murray River. Those towns can still be visited today, with their historic buildings and German flavor.

Several copper mines were discovered in South Australia in the late 1800s, too. Such new discoveries always caused a lot of excitement.

And finally, the unwelcome locust plague actually happened across much of southern Australia in the late 1800s. Thousands of acres of cropland were devoured by these clouds of hungry insects. It made life especially tough for the farmers and settlers, people who depended on the land. And if they'd ever thought about giving up and going home (wherever "home" might have been), it was then. In fact, the plagues were so severe that in 1872 the government of South Australia declared an official day of "humiliation and prayer" throughout the Riverina District. (Remember the pastor reading that proclamation in church? Those were the actual words.) Sadly, those kinds of proclamations would probably never be issued today—even if the locusts returned.

In any case, Patrick and his family, like other hardy Australian pioneers, learned some tough lessons about how to make a new home. For one thing, they learned to get along with people very different from themselves. And they learned to trust God despite all the obstacles—droughts, floods, plagues, hard work, even loneliness. And though Patrick at first thought he'd rather return to Ireland, he grew up to learn that he had not really left his home—he had found it.

Series for Middle Graders* From BHP

ADVENTURES DOWN UNDER · by Robert Elmer
When Patrick McWaid's father is unjustly sent to Australia as a prisoner in 1867, the rest of the family follows, uncovering action-packed mystery along the way.

ADVENTURES OF THE NORTHWOODS · by Lois Walfrid Johnson
Kate O'Connell and her stepbrother Anders encounter mystery and adventure in northwest Wisconsin near the turn of the century.

AN AMERICAN ADVENTURE SERIES · by Lee Roddy
Hildy Corrigan and her family must overcome danger and hardship during the Great Depression as they search for a "forever home."

BLOODHOUNDS, INC. · by Bill Myers
Hilarious, hair-raising suspense follows brother-and-sister detectives Sean and Melissa Hunter in these madcap mysteries with a message.

GIRLS ONLY! · by Beverly Lewis
Four talented young athletes become fast friends as together they pursue their Olympic dreams.

JOURNEYS TO FAYRAH · by Bill Myers
Join Denise, Nathan, and Josh on amazing journeys as they discover the wonders and lessons of the mystical Kingdom of Fayrah.

MANDIE BOOKS · by Lois Gladys Leppard
With over four million sold, the turn-of-the-century adventures of Mandie and her many friends will keep readers eager for more.

THE RIVERBOAT ADVENTURES · by Lois Walfrid Johnson
Libby Norstad and her friend Caleb face the challenges and risks of working with the Underground Railroad during the mid–1800s.

TRAILBLAZER BOOKS · by Dave and Neta Jackson
Follow the exciting lives of real-life Christian heroes through the eyes of child characters as they share their faith with others around the world.

THE TWELVE CANDLES CLUB · by Elaine L. Schulte
When four twelve-year-old girls set up a business of odd jobs and babysitting, they uncover wacky adventures and hilarious surprises.

THE YOUNG UNDERGROUND · by Robert Elmer
Peter and Elise Andersen's plots to protect their friends and themselves from Nazi soldiers in World War II Denmark guarantee fast-paced action and suspenseful reads.

*(ages 8–13)